"Phoebe?" Piper

"Phoebe! If y   anything!" Paige called.

They came around the corner into a dead-end alley. A chill went right through Paige. It was deserted, but she had this strong feeling that her sister had been there. She raced to the end of the alley and checked behind crates and garbage bins, dreading at every second that she was going to find her sister knocked out—or worse. There was no sign of Phoebe. Paige wasn't sure whether to be relieved, or even more frightened.

"She's not here," she said, throwing out her arms.

Piper slowly walked toward Paige, looking at the ground. "Yeah, but she was," she said. "Look."

Paige joined her sister and stared down at the asphalt. There was a huge, black scorch mark right in the center of the alley. She swallowed hard, then shivered. Hugging herself, she looked at Piper.

"Well. At least she vanquished him," she said.

"Yeah, but that still doesn't explain where *she* is," Piper pointed out. "Can you sense her?"

Paige took a deep breath. *Talk about pressure.* She closed her eyes and tapped into her Whitelighter powers. She tried to reach out, tried to feel her sister, but she was too distracted. Too distracted by this overwhelming feeling of dread. She sensed nothing. A big, empty, cold nothing.

Charmed®

Published by Simon & Schuster

PHOEBE WHO?

PHOEBE WHO?

An original novel by Emma Harrison

Based on the hit TV series created by

Constance M. Burge

SIMON SPOTLIGHT ENTERTAINMENT
New York   London   Toronto   Sydney

This book is a work of fiction. Any references to historical events, real people, or real locales are used fictitiously. Other names, characters, places, and incidents are the product of the author's imagination, and any resemblance to actual events or locales or persons, living or dead, is entirely coincidental.

S|S|E

SIMON SPOTLIGHT ENTERTAINMENT
An imprint of Simon & Schuster Children's Publishing Division
1230 Avenue of the Americas, New York, New York 10020
® and © 2006 Spelling Television Inc. A CBS Company. All Rights Reserved.
All rights reserved, including the right of reproduction in whole or in part in any form.
SIMON SPOTLIGHT ENTERTAINMENT and related logo are trademarks of Simon & Schuster, Inc.
Manufactured in the United States of America
First Edition 10 9 8 7 6 5 4 3 2 1
Library of Congress Control Number 2006925836
ISBN-13: 978-1-4169-2532-3
ISBN-10: 1-4169-2532-5

For Holly Marie, Alyssa, Rose, and Brian:
We'll miss you!

Chapter 1

"I'm sorry. There's just no way I'll have time to meet you for an interview today," Phoebe Halliwell said into her office phone, balancing the receiver against her shoulder as she typed. "I'm swamped over here."

Her other line began to ring and she lifted her head to check the caller ID. Her neck instantly twinged with pain. She grimaced, rubbing at her strained muscle. Apparently she had been in that position for far too long. One of these days her neck was going to stick like that and she was going to walk out of the *Bay Mirror* offices looking like a deformed zombie. Without the rotting flesh part.

"Then how about a phone interview?" asked the reporter on the other end of the line. "I have the questions all ready. We can do it right now."

Phoebe closed her eyes and tried not to sigh audibly. These people did not take no for an answer. She knew the girl was just trying to do her job, but at the moment, Phoebe was too. And she was getting nowhere.

"I'm sorry, but I really have to finish my column for tomorrow. You know how important my readers are to me. If I let them down, then you guys over there at *Vogue* won't want to do an article on me anymore," she joked, hoping to lighten the mood.

"*Vogue*? I'm from *Marie Claire!*" the interviewer snapped.

Phoebe's face fell right along with her heart. "Uh . . . of course you are. I'm so sorry. It's just been so crazy around here lately. . . ."

Sheesh. How could she have made that mistake? The girl from *Vogue* was the one who had called first thing that morning. The one she had yet to find the time to call back.

"You know what? You just lost your chance at a feature in our magazine," the woman said, clearly irritated.

"I'm really—"

The line went dead and Phoebe slumped back in her chair. "Sorry," she finished.

Frustrated, Phoebe hung up the phone and rubbed her forehead. She breathed in and out deeply, counting to three with each breath, attempting to destress. Although it would have been great for her career to have a feature in *Marie Claire*, she was actually relieved to be off the phone, whatever the consequence. Her other line was still ringing, but she decided to ignore it. She only had fifteen minutes until the final deadline for her column, and this last letter was giving her all kinds of trouble.

Okay. All I need is a little peace and quiet and I can breeze right through this, Phoebe told herself.

She pulled her chair closer to her keyboard and caught a glimpse of her reflection in a compact mirror she'd left open on her desk. It made her flinch. Dark circles under her brown eyes, her light brown hair hanging in limp tendrils around her seriously color-lacking face. Not a pretty sight. What had happened to her hot, young self?

Oh, yeah. She hadn't seen the sun in days and had barely slept for the past few nights. That could erase all vestiges of beauty from a person.

Just finish this and then maybe this weekend you can treat yourself to a massage and a walk around Golden Gate Park, she thought, rounding her shoulders. *Plus a whole lotta beauty sleep.* She placed her hands on her keyboard and started to type.

Dear M

The door to her office burst open.

"What is *this*?" Phoebe's editor, Elyse, cried, holding up a few typed pages.

Elyse's red hair was sticking out on the side and she had one pair of glasses on top of her head and another perched on the end of her nose. Her neck scarf was all askew and she had a ketchup stain on her blazer. Apparently Elyse was having a tough day as well. At least Phoebe's chic white cropped blazer and funky black skirt were still in place and unmarked.

"What is what?" Phoebe groaned, already dreading the answer.

"This!" Elyse looked down at the page. "You told a woman whose boyfriend was just deployed to Iraq to, and I quote, 'Dump the guy. If he's not going to be there for you, then he's not worth your time.'"

Phoebe's eyes widened. "Nooooo," she said, standing and walking around her desk. "No, I wouldn't have said that."

"It's right here! Just about to make its way into tomorrow's paper!" Elyse exclaimed, so shrilly it made Phoebe flinch.

"Can I see that for just a second?" Phoebe asked. She delicately removed the pages from Elyse's clenched fingers and scanned the letter and response.

"Ah! I see what happened here. This was the advice I gave to that girl whose guy told her point-blank that she was number five on his priority list."

"Number five?" Elyse asked.

Phoebe nodded. "After work, his car, his buddies, the 49ers, and his mom."

"Ouch," Elyse said, shaking her head in disgust.   •

"Tell me about it," Phoebe replied.

"Well, I don't have that letter anywhere."

Elyse quickly flipped through her pages, then threw her hands in the air.

"I have it. I mean, I should. It should be on my computer . . . somewhere," Phoebe said. She had so much on her mind just then that she couldn't for the life of her remember where she had stashed the letter. Had she scanned it in? Typed it over on her desktop? Saved it on her laptop, perhaps? Phoebe was drawing a blank. All she knew was that she had read it and answered it. And that somehow it had gotten lost between her computer and Elyse's.

"Well, find it," Elyse told her, checking her watch. "You have ten minutes."

The cell phone in Phoebe's bag started to ring and Elyse gave her an impatient look. Elyse knew from experience that when Phoebe's cell trilled, it was never a good sign. It often meant that Phoebe had to leave work to take care of a "family emergency."

What Elyse didn't know, however, was that in Phoebe's family, an emergency usually meant that someone was in mortal peril, or that the world itself needed saving. On top of her high-pressure job as an advice columnist at the *Bay Mirror*, Phoebe was also one third of the Charmed trio, three sisters who also just happened to be good witches, and who spent any and all of their "free time" battling the forces of evil. Along with her older sister Piper and her younger half sister Paige Matthews, Phoebe had prevented total global destruction on more than a few occasions. She just hoped that this phone call wouldn't result in another epic battle. Not when she had a deadline looming.

"I know. Ten minutes," Phoebe said.

"*Ten*," Elyse said pointedly. Then she walked out, leaving the door open, and Phoebe dove for her phone. The caller ID read, of course, HOME.

"Hello?" Phoebe answered, so tense she could have crushed the tiny cell in one hand.

"Phoebe! Thank God! I've been calling your office line. Where have you been?"

It was Piper. Phoebe's older sister. And she sounded about as impatient as Elyse had looked.

"I've been here. I've just been busy," Phoebe said. "Why? What's wrong?"

"I need you to come home and watch Wyatt," Piper said. "Leo's stuck with the elders and I need to get to P3 and balance the accounts or the IRS is going to come down on us worse than any demon ever has."

Phoebe sighed. Well, at least it wasn't the end of the world. Always a bright side. "I know the tax guys are evil, Piper, but I'm totally swamped over here. Can't Paige do it?"

"No. Because Miss Paige is off doing her own thing," Piper said sarcastically. "As always," she added under her breath.

Phoebe's brow knit. "Her own thing?"

Outside her office, across the paper's bull pen area, Elyse crossed her arms over her chest and stared Phoebe down. Phoebe held up one finger and turned her back to Elyse.

"You know, protecting Innocents," Piper said.

"Isn't that what we're *supposed* to do?" Phoebe asked.

"Yeah, but if you ask me, Paige has been doing a little too much of that lately and not enough helping out around here," Piper said. "I can't do everything, you know."

I know the feeling, Phoebe thought as her office phone started to ring again. Lately, Paige and Piper had been very tense with each other, while Paige ran around from temp job to temp job, each of which seemed to have some kind of magical purpose. Piper was getting tired of Paige's lack of focus and her willingness to be called away to strangers' sides at the blink of an eye, while her family needed her at home. Meanwhile, Paige felt that Piper was trying to mother her, to tell her what to do all the time and how to do it. Trying to constantly mediate between the two of them, Phoebe had never felt more like the middle child. It was just one more thing on her list of ten million things to do.

"Okay. I'll be home as soon as I can. I promise," Phoebe told Piper.

"Thank you," Piper said. Phoebe was about to hang up when Piper added. "And bring milk!"

Phoebe closed her phone, then turned and shut her office door to close Elyse out as well.

She took another deep breath and turned to go back to her computer. The moment she did, a rainbow appeared in the center of her office. Phoebe jumped back, startled, as a leprechaun in a green top hat and brown pants slid right down the rainbow to the floor and leaned on his staff.

Good thing I closed the door, Phoebe thought.

"I've got a bone to pick with you," the leprechaun said.

Phoebe rolled her eyes, over the initial shock of her visitor. He was, after all, not the first leprechaun she had ever encountered. Just the first to slide into her office in the middle of a workday.

"Why am I not surprised?" She walked around the little man and sat down at her desk. "What can I do for you?"

"My name is Teague," he said with a slight bow. "And I come as a representative of the magical community. The community that you have been ignoring for far too long."

"Excuse me? My sisters and I fight demons every day of the week," Phoebe replied, as she resumed typing. "I'd hardly call that *ignoring*."

"This is not about demons. It's about advice," Teague said, spreading his arms wide. "Here ya been givin' it out to all these mortals for years like it's common ale. What about the rest of us?"

Phoebe's fingers froze atop her keyboard. "You want *love* advice?" she asked.

Teague's auburn eyebrows came together.

"What? You think I can't get a woman? I'm very popular back on the lea, you know."

Phoebe tried not to laugh. "I'm sure you are." She folded her fingers on top of her desk and looked over its wide, messy expanse at her visitor. "So where do you suggest I publish this advice, exactly? Is there some magical newspaper I don't know about?"

Teague scoffed. "No. 'Course not. We were thinking you could hold some counseling sessions. Talk to us in person."

"Oh, no! No way," Phoebe said, turning back to her computer. "I do not have time to add 'magical relationship counselor' to my résumé. Now, if you'll excuse me, I have a column to write and about three minutes left to write it."

"Suit yourself," Teague said with a shrug. He walked over to her filing cabinet and toyed with the handle on one of the lower drawers. "A' course, there might be some payback if you don't do it. Need I remind you how much havoc fairies and nymphs and giants can cause?"

"Are you threatening me?" Phoebe asked. This was so not what she needed right now.

"A bloke's gotta do what a bloke's gotta do," Teague said. "I go back and tell all those folks you said no, I can't be responsible for their reactions."

Phoebe's shoulders drooped. "There are really that many magical beings who need my help?"

"Enough to send your precious manor into total chaos for at least the next decade," Teague said with a twinkle in his eye. "I'm willing to bet that wouldn't be good for the Charmed Ones' reputation."

Phoebe's temples started to throb at the very idea of taking on something new. Especially something with this much responsibility attached. But if what Teague said were true and the magical world decided to retaliate, she would never hear the end of it from Piper and Paige. She saw her hopes of a relaxing weekend, of her massage and her walk in the park and some decent sleep, evaporate before her eyes.

"Fine," Phoebe said finally. "We'll do it this weekend at the manor."

"A wise decision," Teague said with a tip of his hat. "I'll inform the others. And we'll see *you* on Saturday."

Then he jumped on his rainbow and disappeared.

"Can't wait," Phoebe said, as Elyse began to tap on the door and Phoebe's cell started to ring in unison. "'Cause clearly I have nothing else to do with my time."

Phoebe took the steps up to Halliwell Manor two at a time, struggling with her large tote bag full of books and papers, her laptop bag, and the grocery bags overflowing with food and supplies. Piper had left a message on Phoebe's voicemail with a list of things to pick up along with the milk. All together it was just enough to put Phoebe over the express-line limit, which had made her even later. She grasped at the front doorknob and twisted it just enough to hear a click, then shoved her way inside and slammed the door with her designer shoe.

"Hey! Sorry I'm late!" she called out, her voice carrying throughout the large Victorian house.

"We're in here!" Piper shouted back from the kitchen.

Phoebe tromped through the dining room, past the antique table and chairs, and into the kitchen where her older sister was just lifting baby Wyatt out of his high chair.

"Hey," Piper said.

"I'm so, *so* sorry. I had to find this letter for Elyse, and then she made me rewrite my last reply. It was totally insane."

Phoebe dropped the grocery bags onto the counter, turned around, and immediately found Wyatt in her arms.

"Don't worry about it," Piper said, grabbing her keys. "Gotta go!"

She leaned down to kiss Wyatt on top of his head, her long dark hair swinging behind her. Phoebe watched as her sister gathered up her purse and a folder bulging with papers, then headed for the door.

"Oh! Wait! I forgot to tell you," Piper said,

whirling around again. "There are a couple of pictures missing from the house."

Phoebe adjusted Wyatt in her arms and blinked. "Pictures?"

"From the hallway. One of the three of us. And one of you and Dad," Piper said.

"Did we have a break-in or something?" Phoebe asked, alarmed.

"Possibly. And if they're taking photos then it's one of two things: a stalker or some kind of voodoo witchcraft thing," Piper said. "So keep an eye out."

Once again, Piper turned to go.

"Wait! That's it?" Phoebe asked as Wyatt reached up and grabbed her hair. Phoebe winced and tried to disentangle his fingers. "Aren't you at all worried about this?"

"Of course I am," Piper said impatiently. "But there's nothing I can do about it right now. Right *now*, I have to deal with my business. If something happens, we'll deal with it then."

With that, she turned on her heel and finally made it all the way through the door.

"You're welcome!" Phoebe shouted after her.

Phoebe looked down at little blond Wyatt, who had stuffed his hand into his mouth. He stared back with big, curious blue eyes.

"Hi, baby! You're getting heavier every day, you know that?" she said in her best sweet-auntie voice.

Her purse straps were sliding down her arms

and she needed to find someplace to rest Wyatt so she could drop the rest of her stuff and then put the groceries away. But the tiny tray was still attached to the high chair, making it impossible to plop him down, and there was nowhere else in the kitchen to rest him.

Phoebe was about to head toward the sun-room and Wyatt's playpen when Paige orbed in right in the center of the kitchen, white light swirling all around her. For the millionth time, Phoebe wished she could orb. She would have been home a lot faster if she could. But Paige's dad had been a Whitelighter, while Phoebe's had been but a human. So, no cool transporta-tion tricks for Phoebe.

Still, it was nice to have a sister who could do it. Especially at times like these.

"Paige! Great! You're here!" Phoebe said, holding Wyatt out. "You can help. I have all this work to finish up and Wyatt needs to be put down to sleep and—"

"Sorry, Phoebe. No can do!" Paige said, traips-ing over to the potion cabinet. She reached inside and pulled out a red vial. "There's a lower-level demon after Mikey, and I need to do some van-quishing," she said with a quick, determined nod.

"Mikey?" Phoebe said, struggling to transfer Wyatt to her other arm.

"The kid I've been tutoring?" Paige reminded her. "I think he may be a future Whitelighter, and that was why I was sent to him. Anyway, I just came home to get a potion," she said, giving the vial a quick shake.

"Oh. Well, is there anything I can do?" Phoebe asked, an automatic reflex. In truth, there wasn't much she could have done to help, what with all the other helping she was already doing.

"No, thanks," Paige replied. She reached back and pulled her dark hair up into a ponytail, all the better for demon hunting. "I've got it under control."

At that moment, Wyatt turned his head and burped up orange goo all over Phoebe's laptop bag. Phoebe closed her eyes, her nose scrunching against the smell.

"Oooh. That's gonna leave a stain," Paige said.

Phoebe groaned. "I need a vacation."

"Who doesn't?" Paige joked. Then she waved merrily and orbed out.

"Yeah. You look really stressed," Phoebe said to the empty kitchen. Wyatt started to cry and Phoebe bounced him up and down. "It's okay. You're okay," she told him. "Come on. Let's go get you cleaned up." She looked down at her dripping laptop bag. "And then maybe we'll clean *me* up."

Piper sat in her office at P3, the dance club and bar she owned and operated, poring over the books she had ignored for far too long. Her assistant manager, Pete, was supposed to be keeping everything updated, but apparently he had been slacking quite a bit. He hadn't balanced the checkbook in two months, and there were bills outstanding from last Christmas. Piper hit a few buttons on her calculator and made an entry in her ledger.

"If you want something done right, you've gotta do it yourself," she muttered aloud, making a mental note to fire Pete. She looked up at the hundreds of posters of bands and acts that papered the walls of her office. "But you already knew that, didn't you, Madonna?" she asked the picture of the blonde bombshell directly in front of her. Then she smirked to herself and got back to work.

Out of nowhere, a huge crash sounded from the deserted club. Piper looked up, her heart pounding. This could not be good.

"Piper!" someone shouted.

It was Paige. Another crash. Piper was on her feet and out the door, hands raised and ready for action. She ran out among the cocktail tables and saw her sister crouched on the floor on one side of the large, round bar, while three mangy-looking demons in ragged coats and beards shot fireballs at her from the other side.

"What's going on?" Piper asked.

"A little help?" Paige said, ducking as another fireball shot by.

Piper raised her hands and shot her power at

one of the offending demons. He was blasted
back against the wall, stunned, but he didn't
explode. Piper hesitated for a moment. Usually
when she unleashed her firepower on a demon,
he exploded. Unless the demon himself was
superpowerful.

"What's the matter? Hit the other ones!"
Paige cried.

"All right! All right!" Piper said. She hit the
second, then the third, with the same results.
Then the first demon got up and flung a fireball
right at her. Piper let out a screech and dove
down next to Paige.

"Who *are* these guys?" she asked, shoving her
hair out of her face.

"I don't know!" Paige wailed. "I thought
there was just one of them, but obviously I was
wrong."

"Well, they're immune to my powers," Piper
told her, sitting up straight, her back against
the bar.

"Dammit. They can't be lower-level then,"
Paige said.

"You're fighting these guys and you know
nothing about them?" Piper scolded. "Didn't
you even check the Book of Shadows?"

The Book of Shadows was the Charmed
Ones' magical guidebook. It had been passed
down from generation to generation and con-
tained information on almost every demon
the sisters had ever come up against, as well as

hundreds of useful spells and potions. Piper was a stickler when it came to checking the Book.

Paige rolled her eyes. "Sorry, *Mom*. I *thought* I knew what I was doing."

"Yeah, well, apparently you didn't," Piper shot back.

"Come out, come out, wherever you are!" one of the demons taunted, earning a round of laughter from his buddies. A fireball zoomed by overhead and took out one of the alcove booths in the corner.

"Hey, at least I came to you for help this time," Paige said, irritated. "Isn't that one of your many complaints? That I'm always trying to do things by myself?"

Another booth exploded, sending shards of destroyed table flying in all directions.

"Well, thanks so much for bringing them to my club!" Piper said.

"I'm sorry, but I didn't know where else to go," Paige said through her teeth. "Besides, how did I know they were gonna be able to follow me? I *orbed* here. They shimmered in two seconds after me."

"Crafty little suckers," Piper said.

Another fireball, then another, zipped past them, taking out tables and chairs and scorching the dance floor.

"All right. That's it!" Piper cried, jumping up.

She blasted each of the demons again, one at a time, sending them flying all over the club, crashing into walls and tables. Paige stood up next to her.

"Go get Phoebe," Piper ordered, leveling one of the demons as he tried to get up. Finally, and much to Piper's surprise, he was engulfed in hellfire and incinerated. Apparently, the third time was the charm.

"Are you sure?" Paige said, breathless.

"Yes! We might need the Power of Three here. I can fend them off until you get back," Piper told her. There was another blast, which resulted in a cracked wall and a shattered light fixture. Piper tried to block the image of the repair bill from her mind. "Just go!"

Paige orbed out, leaving Piper to fight—for the moment—alone.

Chapter 2

"I know, Wyatt. I know," Phoebe cooed, bouncing her nephew in her lap. She held him around his stomach with her left hand, his pudgy legs straddling her knee, while typing on her laptop with her right. All she could do was hope that he didn't barf again—because if he did, this time he'd be doing it all over her keyboard. "I know you don't like that itchy shirt, but nothing else was clean."

Phoebe looked down at Wyatt's red face, a single tear stuck to the middle of his plump cheek. Maybe she should just take the shirt off altogether. He could sit around half naked until the laundry was done, right? She was about to yank the tiny offending sweater off of him, but then she would run the risk of his catching cold. And she did not want to be responsible for making Wyatt sick.

Checking her watch, Phoebe kissed Wyatt on the temple. "Just a couple more minutes and the

laundry will be dry," she said. "Apparently
Mommy fell behind on the wash. Which, of
course, she forgot to tell me about."

Wyatt cried louder and Phoebe felt a stab of
guilt. "Not that I'm blaming Mommy. No!" she
said, shaking her head. "No! Mommy loves you!
She was just busy today!"

Wyatt continued to wail, and Phoebe felt as if
she were about to burst. She finally gave up on
her column and stood, hoisting him up into her
arms.

"It's okay, honey. No, don't cry! It's okay!"
she sang to him, walking him around the dark-
ened sunroom.

"Ooooh . . . where is Paige?" she wondered
aloud. There was nothing like a baby's cry to get
under her skin and make her feel desperate. "I
could use a little help around here!" she said
loudly, hoping Leo or Paige or *someone* would
hear her and come to help. But the baby cavalry
didn't come orbing into the room. The only
reply to her plea was Wyatt's sobbing.

"Come on, baby! What can I do to make you
stop crying?" Phoebe asked.

Then the buzzer went off on the dryer in the
basement. Relief flooded through her.

"See? There we go, Wyatt!" Phoebe said,
hightailing it for the kitchen and the basement
beyond. "We'll get you out of that scratchy shirt
in no time!"

She flicked on the light and started down the

steps. Every time she went down to the basement these days, she had to smile, remembering
how, as a kid, she had been afraid of the lowest
floor of the manor. In fact, the "irrational" fear
had lasted until she was in her early twenties, a
fact that always embarrassed her. Of course, she
hadn't found out until then that her fears were
completely founded. A supernatural force called
the Woogie resided underneath the floor of the
basement, and Phoebe had seen it trying to
attack her grandmother when she was very
little. Now that she and her sisters had vanquished it, however, Phoebe had accomplished
something that no one else had ever done: She
had literally conquered her childhood fear.

Halfway down the stairs, Paige and Leo
orbed in right in front of her. Phoebe's heart flew
into her throat and she grabbed the banister,
holding on to Wyatt with her other arm.

"Oh! A little warning, please?" she said, glaring at the two of them.

Okay. So maybe the basement-related jumpi-
ness wasn't completely gone.

"Sorry," Leo said with a shrug. His handsome
face was lined with concern and his blue eyes
shot to Wyatt, who was still crying. Ever the pro-
tective father. "Here. Let me take him." Leo
reached out for his son and Phoebe handed him
over, all her senses on alert.

"Come on. We have to go," Paige said. Her
white blouse had burn marks all over it.

"Are you okay? What's wrong?" Phoebe asked, as her sister pulled her back upstairs.

"It's Piper. She's under attack," Leo told her.

"Attack? By who?" Phoebe asked.

"Remember that lower-level demon I thought was after Mikey?" Paige asked. She yanked open the cabinet and pulled down potion after potion, handing a few to Phoebe. "Turns out he wasn't lower-level *and* he wasn't alone. Plus, it seems he was after *me*."

"Who are they?" Phoebe asked.

"I have no idea. We just have to go. Piper needs us."

"I'll take care of Wyatt," Leo told Phoebe.

"He needs a new shirt!" Phoebe called out to Leo, remembering at the last second.

As Paige orbed Phoebe out of the manor, all she saw in front of her was Leo's grim face.

The moment Phoebe appeared in the center of the P3 dance floor, an energy ball zoomed past her head, so close that her skin sizzled and her hair was charged with static.

"Run!" Piper screamed at the top of her lungs, heading for the back door.

Phoebe and Paige immediately gave chase. Another energy ball exploded just behind them, knocking Paige off her feet. Phoebe grabbed her sister's arm and pulled her up. As they scurried out the back door and into the alley, Phoebe got a quick look at their attackers. There were three of them, each with a long beard of a different color, and bright yellow eyes that glowed with malice.

"What's going on?" Paige cried as the three sisters took cover behind a Dumpster. "I thought you killed one of them!"

"I did! I had to hit him three times, but it worked. Unfortunately, he had backup," Piper said, checking a scrape on her arm. "In fact, it's like they have an endless stream of backups. Every time you kill one, another one shimmers in to take its place a couple minutes later."

"They *do* have an endless stream of backups. Well, almost endless," Phoebe confirmed, crouching on the wet, silty asphalt.

"You know what they are?" Piper asked.

"I've seen them in the Book," Phoebe said with a nod. "They're Flecter demons."

"Well, how do we kill them?" Paige asked as the back door they had come through burst open.

Phoebe flinched. "We can't. They're invincible unless you kill the emperor. Then, apparently, they all go *poof.*"

"We know you're out here!" one of the demons shouted. "We can *smell* you."

"Well, which one is the emperor?" Piper demanded.

"I don't know *everything,*" Phoebe told her.

An energy ball decimated a garbage can across the alley, sending heaps of trash everywhere.

Phoebe covered her head with her arms as she
and her sisters huddled together.

"You thinking what I'm thinking?" Phoebe
asked them.

"Divide and conquer?" Paige said, pursing
her lips.

"Sounds like a plan," Piper said. "On the
count of three. One . . . two . . . three!"

Phoebe squeezed Paige's hand once before
jumping up and running for her life. She dodged
one energy ball and glanced over her shoulder
as Piper stood up and started blasting away.

She's okay. She's going to be okay, she thought.

Then another energy ball smacked into the
wall next to Phoebe's head and she took off,
racing around the corner and into the next alley.
She knew from experience that if she had to
make a quick exit, she could levitate to the fire
escape above the Chinese restaurant, then climb
to the roof and jump down to the lower building
on the other side. A few battles had taken place
here before.

Phoebe paused in the center of the alley, a
seeming dead end, and reached into her pants
pocket for one of the vanquishing potions. She
turned and waited for her demon to come and
get her. When he stepped into the alley, he
grinned broadly, showing off yellow, pointed
teeth beneath his red beard.

"Nowhere else to run, witch," he said, spitting everywhere.

"I'm done running," Phoebe replied, her heart pounding in her ears.

"Good." The demon shimmered out and Phoebe's breath caught in her throat. She whirled around, just as he reappeared right behind her. He grabbed her by the neck with his rough, dirty hand and shoved her backward against the wall. As soon as she hit the wall, the vanquishing potion slipped from her fingers and tumbled to the ground.

"Let's have a little fun," the demon said, easily lifting her into the air.

Sputtering for breath, Phoebe lifted both knees in one swift motion and slammed them into the demon's chin. His head snapped back and he stumbled, dropping Phoebe to the ground. She landed on her butt, but jumped right to her feet, assuming a fighting stance. The demon threw a punch, which Phoebe easily blocked. She kicked him away, then hit him with a nice upper kick while he was still reeling. The demon grunted in surprise and fell flat on his back.

Phoebe grabbed up her vanquishing potion and stepped over him. The demon's chest rose and fell with a shudder. He stared straight up at the sky with his yellow eyes, stunned.

"Fun enough for you?" Phoebe asked.

She pulled back and smashed the bottle of vanquishing potion at his feet. Instantly, the demon started to smoke. He writhed and jerked and screeched as fire consumed him. Phoebe quickly backed up, but not quite fast enough. With a burst of white-hot light, the demon exploded into the ether. Phoebe threw her arms up and ducked, but the force of the explosion blew her off her feet.

This was going to hurt.

Phoebe braced herself as she went airborne and her stomach swooped against gravity. Two seconds later, her head smacked against the grainy surface of the brick wall, followed by her back and legs. Every bone in her body was jarred. But, as she slipped to the ground, she knew she was okay. There was going to be a lot of pain tomorrow, but she was okay.

Until another blast hit her. Square in the face. Something warm, then hot, then freezing. Something undeniably magical. Something that made her blood run cold.

"What the—" Phoebe said dizzily.

The alley tilted in front of her. Her eyes refused to focus. She heard footsteps echoing through the darkness, but they sounded far, far away. Dimly, she thought her sisters might be coming for her. Then she saw a pair of strappy sandals, an ankle tattoo. Not her sisters. Someone else. And then everything went fuzzy. And then everything went black.

After vanquishing the black-bearded demon with her potion, Paige orbed back to the alley behind P3 to help Piper. The second she arrived, she had to orb again, to avoid a renegade energy ball. She reappeared behind the Dumpster and crouched there as explosions popped all around her. Piper jumped up from her hiding place behind the line of garbage cans and slammed the demon with her power, then ducked down again to avoid another ball.

"How many times have you hit him?" Paige yelled.

"Twice!" Piper replied. "I think!" She stood up again and ran to join Paige, but dropped to the ground on her stomach in the center of the alley as an energy ball zipped past her. She pressed her hands into the blacktop at her sides.

"Ha! Try once!" the demon taunted her.

"Here. This works," Paige told Piper, rolling a vanquishing potion across the dirty alley floor to Piper. "And nobody came to back him up."

"Sounds good to me," Piper said, laying her hand flat over the bottle.

The demon chuckled and walked toward Piper. "Oh. What do you have there? A little potion?" he asked, his yellow eyes gleaming.

Piper looked up at him over her shoulder just as he formed another energy ball between his hands. He lifted it over his head as Piper flipped over. The girl was a sitting duck. Or a lying-on-her-back duck.

"Energy ball!" Paige shouted, thrusting out her hand.

Instantly, the ball of white fire disappeared in a swirl of orbs, then reappeared, hovering above Paige's hands. The demon looked up, confused, giving Piper just enough time to roll away. She stood up and tossed the potion to the ground at his feet.

"Huh?" the demon said.

"Gotcha," Piper told him, crossing her arms over her chest.

"You might wanna take cover," Paige said, recalling the dramatic way in which her own demon had met his bitter end. She waved Piper over with her free hand.

Piper dove behind the Dumpster just as the demon screamed and burst into flames. A hot wind blew Paige's hair back as Piper ducked her head behind her sister's shoulder.

"Well. Guess I won't be needing this," Paige said, pulling her arm back.

"Don't!" Piper shouted.

But it was too late. Paige had already let the energy ball fly, tossing it at the wall across from them. It took out another garbage can with a *bang*, littering the alley with rotting food. A banana peel fell right on top of Paige's new sandal. Totally disgusting.

"Nice work," Piper said facetiously, pushing herself to her feet. She removed a few orange rinds from her blouse with her fingertips and flicked them to the ground.

"Sorry. What did you want me to do with it?"

Paige said as she brushed off her black pants and kicked the banana peel free.

"I don't know. Throw it at something I wouldn't have to clean up later?" Piper said.

"Why are you all over me lately?" Paige asked, irritated.

"Is it so much to ask that you think before you act?" Piper demanded. "It's like you're regressing or something."

"I am not regressing!" Paige shot back. "I am just trying to live my life," she added, placing her hand on her chest. "And if you would just—"

"Wait a second!" Piper said, lifting a hand.

"What!?" Paige said through her teeth, annoyed at being cut off.

"Do you hear that?" Piper asked.

Paige listened. She heard nothing but the traffic out on the street beyond the alley. "No. I hear nothing."

"Exactly," Piper said.

Paige's heart thumped extrahard. "Phoebe."

The silence might have been a good sign if Phoebe had vanquished her demon as well. But if she *had*, then where was she? She should have come right back to P3 to let her sisters know that she was okay.

Paige and Piper exchanged alarmed looks. Together, they bolted out of the alley, following Phoebe's earlier footsteps.

"Phoebe?" Piper shouted. "Phoebe! Where are you?"

"Phoebe! If you can hear us, just . . . shout. Shout anything!" Paige called.

They came around the corner into a dead-end alley. A chill went right through Paige. It was deserted, but she had this strong feeling that her sister had been there. She raced to the end of the alley and checked behind crates and garbage bins, dreading at every second that she was going to find her sister knocked out—or worse. There was no sign of Phoebe. Paige wasn't sure whether to be relieved, or even more frightened.

"She's not here," she said, throwing out her arms.

Piper slowly walked toward Paige, looking at the ground. "Yeah, but she was," she said. "Look."

Paige joined her sister and stared down at the asphalt. There was a huge, black scorch mark right in the center of the alley. She swallowed hard, then shivered. Hugging herself, she looked at Piper.

"Well. At least she vanquished him," she said.

"Yeah, but that still doesn't explain where *she* is," Piper pointed out. "Can you sense her?"

Paige took a deep breath. *Talk about pressure.* She closed her eyes and tapped into her Whitelighter powers. She tried to reach out, tried to feel her sister, but she was too distracted. Too consumed with this overwhelming feeling of dread. She sensed nothing. A big, empty, cold nothing.

"No," she said finally. "But you know I'm still working on that particular power."

"Maybe we should call Leo," Piper said.

"Leo's with Wyatt," Paige reminded her.

"So, what should we do?" Piper asked, sounding a bit freaked out. Freaked out enough to throw even Paige.

No. We can't lose it. Not yet, Paige told herself. She lifted her chin. There was no way she was going to get all defeatist about this. It wouldn't do them any good.

"Come on. She has to be here somewhere. She's probably just looking for us," she said. "Should we split up and search?"

"No. Let's stay together," Piper said, looking around warily. "I'm not letting *you* out of my sight."

Paige nodded sadly. For once, she didn't mind Piper's mothering instinct. There was something wrong about this. Something very, very wrong.

"Okay. Let's go," she said, not wanting to stay in this eerie dead end a second longer. "Phoebe!" she shouted, leading the way out of the alley. "Phoebe! Answer us!"

Come on, Phoebe, Paige thought. *Where are you?*

Chapter 3

The first thing she felt was pain. Pain in her back and in her legs, but mostly pain in her head. Her skull radiated with it from the inside out, pulsing at a regular beat. She blinked her eyes open and tears rolled from the corners. She wiped them with her fingertips and looked around, wincing each time she turned her head. The ground beneath her was cold and she was surrounded by dark concrete walls and grime. She pushed herself up to a seated position and waited for the head-rush to clear.

Where was she? How had she ended up here?

Okay, just think, she told herself, lifting her chin and looking up at a sliver of purple sky. *What's the last thing you remember?*

She concentrated and tried to think back. Tried to recall something. A place, a person, a face. Anything. But her mind was a complete blank. There was nothing but darkness. The strain of concentrating made her head ache even worse.

How is this possible? How can I remember absolutely nothing?

A shiver ran through her. She carefully got to her knees, then stood up. For a moment, her mind went fuzzy. She pressed her hand against the wall to steady herself. She looked around, trying to find something familiar, but the area around her was devoid of detail. No windows, no signs, not even a random scrap of newspaper or garbage. Nothing but silence. She was alone. A chill wind whistled by and tossed her hair around her face. Another shiver, this one more intense.

She had to get out of here. Now.

Staggering toward an opening at the end of the alley, she glanced around, wondering which way to go. Right or left? Which way would bring her somewhere familiar, somewhere safe?

Home. I have to get home.

But where was that? Try as she might, she couldn't see it. How could she not know where she lived?

Heart pounding, she leaned back against the wall and attempted to breathe.

Okay. Come on. I know where I live. I'm . . . I'm . . .

The world screeched to a stop. Her hand flew to her chest.

I don't even know who I am!

Concentrating as hard as she could through all the pain, she tried to think back. Tried to remember something. Anything. She had to at least know her name! But all she found was emptiness.

Panic started to eat at her veins, but she couldn't let it take over. She needed to find help. But where? From whom? How could she ask for help finding her way when she didn't even know her own name? Where to begin?

Picking a direction at random, she turned left into the alleyway and staggered forward, her mind reeling. How could she not even know who she was? Where she was? How she came to be here? Her hand trailed along the wall as she walked, wanting to hold on to something real. She came to another alleyway, this one lined by metal doors with restaurant and shop names painted on them in block letters. She raced for the first one, hoping it might jog her memory.

"Aldo's," she said. At least she now knew she could read. But the name meant nothing to her. She yanked on the door anyway, desperate. It was locked.

Staggering, she tried the next door, marked SHEETS AND STUFF. Also locked. Her heart was pounding at an insane level now, causing her breath to quicken and her skin to overheat.

Where was she? Why was there no one here? Couldn't anyone help her?

A car horn honked somewhere nearby and she turned around. Traffic! A street! People walking by on the sidewalk. She jogged toward the end of the alley and came out onto a bustling strip of upscale shops, her head pounding mercilessly. A teenage girl and her mother stepped aside, looking at her with concern as she stepped shakily forward. She read the street signs, but she didn't recognize any of the names. She stared at an ad for soap on the side of a bus shelter. Nothing. Nothing at all looked familiar.

Oh, God, oh, God! I don't know anyone. No one knows me. What am I going to do?

Suddenly feeling weak in the knees, she made her way along the busy sidewalk and grabbed the back of a bench next to the bus shelter. Cars whizzed by, kicking up dust, their engines sounding more like roars. Another horn honked, and she felt dizzier still. There was too much going on. She felt as if her brain were spinning in circles.

Slowly, she worked her way around the bench and sat down, putting her head between her knees. She breathed in and out, in and out. She had to get ahold of herself. She had to figure out what had happened to her—and what to do next.

"Ruth? Ruth! Oh, my God! It *is* you! Thank God!"

"Ruth?" she repeated. The name felt strange on her tongue.

Someone grabbed her hands and dropped down, crouching in front of her. She looked up into the dark eyes of the pretty brunette who knelt at the curb. The girl had long hair and wore a flowing aqua blouse over a long skirt and sandals. There was a small braid worked into

her hair near one ear and entwined with a
ribbon. Her expression was both concerned and
relieved.

"Are you okay?" the girl asked, hugging her.
She smelled of lavender. Odd that "Ruth" could
place this particular scent yet hadn't a clue what
city she was in or what her birthday was.
"Where have you been? We've been looking all
over for you."

"Do I know you?"

"What do you mean, do you know me?" the
girl said, leaning back. "This is no time for jokes,
Ruth. The girls are searching all over the
neighborhood for you. We've been so . . ."
Her dark eyes widened. "Oh, my gosh! You're
bleeding!

"I am?" She suddenly felt the cool wetness on
the back of her neck and reached back to touch
it. Her fingertips came away sticky and red. For
some reason this didn't alarm her much. It was
nothing compared to the fact that she hadn't a
clue who she was.

"Ruth, what happened to you? Were you
attacked? Did someone hurt you?" the girl said,
clutching her hands.

"Maybe. I don't know," she said, trying as
hard as she could to remember who Ruth was.
There was still nothing but blackness. Endless
blackness. "Are you sure that's my name?
Ruth?"

"Okay. Now you're *really* starting to scare

me," the girl said. "What's the last thing you remember?"

Ruth narrowed her eyes and wracked her brain. "Waking up. Being cold. Lots of pain. Walking here. That's . . . that's it."

"Oh, my God," the girl said. She got up shakily and sat down on the bench next to Ruth. "So you really don't know me?"

The girl's dozens of bracelets jangled each time she moved. Something about the sound was comforting. Maybe it was familiar. The thought filled Ruth's heart with hope. Could she be remembering something?

She stared at the girl and shook her head slowly, hoping for a twinge of recognition, but none came. "I'm sorry. I don't think so. No."

"I don't believe this. You have amnesia," the girl said. "How could this have happened?"

"I have no idea," Ruth told her.

"Well, let's get you home and clean that up," the girl said, glancing at the back of Ruth's head and grimacing. "Maybe if you see the house you'll remember something."

"The house? Do I live near here?" Ruth asked.

"*We* live near here," the girl said firmly. "Together. We're roommates, remember? We share a house with Delilah and Terra?"

Ruth shook her head. There was nothing familiar about those names. "What about you? What's your name?"

The girl snorted a laugh. "Sorry," she said.

"This is just too weird. I'm Aura," she said, touching her hand to her chest. "You've known me your entire life."

"Really?"

Even though she had no recollection of the girl, this news came as a relief to Ruth. She wasn't alone. She had friends. People who cared about her. Roommates who had been looking for her. That was, if this girl was telling the truth. But what reason could she possibly have for lying? What young woman would pick up a strange, bleeding person from the street and start calling her Ruth? She had to be on the up-and-up.

"Yes, really," Aura replied. She stood up and offered her hand. "Now come on. Once you see the girls and your room, everything will come back to you. I'm sure of it."

A car whizzed by, its stereo blaring. Something inside of Ruth said to be wary of strangers, which this girl technically was. To not be so trusting. But what was she supposed to do? *Everyone* was a stranger. Plus, this girl was offering a way to get off this crazy street. A place to relax and regroup and maybe even figure out this mess. Now was not a time to be overly cautious.

"Okay," Ruth said finally. "Lead the way."

"The girls are going to be so relieved to see you," Aura said, slipping her slim arm around Ruth's shoulders to help her stand. She gave

Ruth a squeeze, then whipped out a cell phone and hit one of the speed-dial buttons. "Dee?" she said into the phone. "I found her. Yes! She's fine. Well, not *totally* fine," she added, shooting Ruth an apologetic smile. "I'll explain when we get home. Are you there already? Cool. We'll be back in a little while."

She snapped the phone shut and reached out her hand. "Come on," she said. "Let's get you home."

Ruth smiled, feeling ten times calmer than when she'd awoken. At least now she had a destination. A place to go. A friendly face to take her there.

"Sounds good to me."

"Wow! This place is beautiful!" Ruth said as she stepped along the Spanish tile path that led to the Craftsman-style home before her. The arched wooden door was framed by two palm trees that bowed toward each other, forming a kind of archway. The walls were white stucco and the roof was made of terra-cotta tiles. Under the moonlight, the house glowed in a welcoming way. She couldn't believe she actually lived here.

"Thanks! We like it," Aura said. "Does it bring back anything for you?"

"No, I can't say that it does," Ruth said, disappointed.

"Well, maybe once you're inside . . . ," Aura said.

She used an old-fashioned iron key to open the door. It creaked as it was pushed open. She held the door for Ruth.

"Welcome to your humble abode," she said with a smile.

"Thank you," Ruth replied cautiously.

The instant Ruth stepped over the threshold, her skin sizzled. It was as if a zap of electricity had shot right through her. She tripped forward, hugging herself. She looked back at the doorway, alarmed, but Aura simply closed and bolted the door as if nothing were out of the ordinary.

"Something wrong?" she asked Ruth.

Ruth didn't want to be impolite, considering this girl was apparently her lifelong friend. Besides, it was probably just her imagination. Some aftereffect of her bump on the head.

"No," she said, forcing a smile. "I'm fine."

"Good. Come on in," Aura said.

She led Ruth through a wide-open foyer with a tiled floor and into a large dining area, centered by a huge raw-oak table with benches on either side. Candles flickered along the length of the table, and an iron candelabrum hung above it. Ruth could smell something sweet and scrumptious baking, and wondered if the kitchen was nearby. Just beyond the dining area was a sunken living room with white couches and tons of pillows.

"It's nice," Ruth said. "But I don't recognize anything."

"Don't pressure yourself," Aura said. "You've

been through a lot. Just relax. Sooner or later it will all come back to you. I swear."

"Okay," Ruth said, taking a deep breath.

Aura turned toward the back of the room and shouted. "Delilah! Terra! We're home!"

Two young women came rushing into the room, completely manic. The first was tall and muscular, with ivory skin and two long, dark braids hanging down her back. She wore a black halter top and black pants, and when she hugged Ruth, she nearly squeezed the air right out of her lungs. Her muscles were solid and taut, as if she worked out all the time. The second girl was much more petite, with light brown skin and curly brown hair highlighted with blonde streaks. Her batik-print skirt danced around her ankles, and she had a diamond piercing in her nose. Her hug was a lot less violent, but no less relieved.

"You're okay!" the second girl trilled, bouncing up and down on bare feet. "You're okay, you're okay, you're okay!"

Ruth pulled away from her slightly, forcing a smile. It was nice that these people were so excited to see her; she just wished she knew who they were. She stared at the two newcomers, hoping for some glimmer of recognition.

"Why are you looking at me like that?" the dark-haired girl asked.

"You guys, I have something to tell you," Aura said calmly. "Ruth has amnesia."

"What?" the petite girl said, her jaw dropping. "No!"

"Yes. She doesn't remember who we are. She doesn't even remember who *she* is. So let's just . . . try to stay calm and help her out," Aura said. "Ruth, this is Delilah," she said, gesturing toward the tall girl. "And that's Terra," she added, pointing to the petite, curly-haired girl.

"Hi," Ruth said. "Nice to . . . meet you, I guess."

"Meet us? You've known us for years!" Terra cried.

"Yes, but she doesn't remember that," Aura told her gently. "Why don't we all just chill out and have something to eat? Whatever you're baking back there smells delicious, Delilah."

"It's your favorite," Delilah told Ruth, looking at her almost warily. "Cranberry muffins."

"Well, why don't you bring them out?" Aura suggested. "And maybe put on some tea."

"Sure. I'm on it," Delilah said, turning to go.

"I don't understand. How did you get amnesia?" Terra asked, her eyes wide.

"It looks like she was hit on the back of the head," Aura told her. "That might have something to do with it.

"Oh, my goddess!" Terra covered her mouth with both hands, noticing Ruth's cut for the first time. "Ouch. Let me get something for that."

Delilah reappeared with a plateful of muffins. The enticing scent filled the room now, and

Ruth's stomach growled. She suddenly felt weak with hunger.

"I'll go get the tea," Aura said. "Sit! Eat!" she told Ruth. "You need your strength."

Ruth sat down on one of the benches, feeling somehow conspicuous now that she and Delilah were alone. She smiled self-consciously and reached for one of the still-steaming muffins.

"Thanks for this," she said.

"No problem," Delilah said, crossing her arms over her chest and lifting one foot onto the bench. "So. You really don't remember anything?"

"No. Sorry," Ruth said with a shrug.

"Weird," Delilah replied. "Where did Aura find you, exactly?"

Ruth glanced down and saw Delilah's sandals. Instantly, she felt a flash of recognition. She had seen those shoes somewhere before, but she couldn't hold the memory in her mind. It flitted away before it had truly formed. Still, considering it was the only thing approaching a memory that she had experienced, it left her heart racing.

"I remember you!" she said, gazing up at Delilah. "At least, I remember your shoes."

Delilah quickly dropped her foot to the floor and sat, tucking her feet under the bench. "Oh, well, you always did have a thing for shoes. Especially mine. You're always borrowing them. Without asking, I might add," she said, narrowing her eyes teasingly.

Ruth blushed. "Sorry. I guess."

"No problem," Delilah said with a shrug.

"So, how long have I known you guys?" Ruth asked, feeling awful for having to ask.

"Well, you've known Aura since you two were kids," Delilah told her. "But Terra and I only met you a few years back. At college."

"College?" Ruth asked.

"UC San Francisco," Delilah told her. "We all graduated together. You majored in English, in case you're wondering. So, do you like the muffin?"

Feeling confused by all this new information, Ruth took a small bite and smiled. The muffin was full of fresh cranberries and laced with cinnamon. "It's amazing," she said.

Delilah's face brightened into a smile. "See? Told you they were your favorite."

"I've got the tea!" Aura announced, returning with a tray lined with mugs and a large black teapot.

"I've got the gauze!" Terra trilled, appearing with a first aid kit.

Aura placed the tray on the table and then stood in front of Ruth, while Terra sat beside her on the bench. Ruth felt gentle fingers cleaning up her cut, then winced slightly as the gauze was taped into place. The whole time Terra worked, Aura and Delilah watched closely. Ruth felt as if she were the main attraction in some medical drama.

"There. Good as new," Terra said happily, patting Ruth's shoulder.

"Thank you."

Then Terra reached behind Ruth for Delilah's hand and Delilah reached out for Aura's. Ruth blinked in surprise as the three girls formed a circle around her and bowed their heads.

"What're you guys doing?"

"Goddess be, protect this, our charge, from harm. Let her not be sought or seen by those who work their charm," the three girls recited.

When they looked up again, all three of them were smiling. "Okay . . . what was that?" Ruth asked.

"We were just asking the goddess to protect you, that's all," Aura said. She picked up the tea tray again and grinned. "Maybe she'll help you remember who you are. Come on. Let's have our tea in the living room."

Ruth stood up, wondering exactly what she had gotten herself into here. Who were these girls? Praying to some goddess? Were they, like, New Agers or something? Did that mean she was into that stuff too? She knew nothing about goddesses or protection chants. But, then again, she didn't even know her own last name.

As she walked into the living room behind the others, Ruth passed by a mirror and paused. *Whoa.* Was that her? Was that what she looked like?

Slowly, she stepped toward her reflection, taking in the limp brown curls around her face, the dark circles under her tired brown eyes. She touched her skin, wondering why it looked so sallow. Apparently, Ruth Whatever-Her-Last-Name-Was hadn't been taking care of herself.

"Come on in and relax," Terra suggested, appearing in the mirror behind her with a bright smile.

Ruth turned away from herself and followed, suddenly feeling exhausted. She sat down near the end of the cushy white couch and sank into the pillows in the corner. As she sat, her eye caught on a framed photo on the table next to the couch. Ruth picked it up for a closer look. In it, she, Aura, Delilah, and Terra stood together in a beautiful fall landscape, their arms thrown around one another, smiling for the camera.

"Wow," Ruth said, a little chill running through her. "When was this taken?"

"Oh, last year, when we went on our annual bike-and-hike in the mountains," Aura said, leaning over her. "You were covered in poison oak after that trip, remember?"

Ruth felt a twinge of discomfort in her chest. "No, I don't," she said apologetically, replacing the picture on the table.

The other three girls exchanged glances, clearly worried. "Well, you will," Terra said. "Maybe you just need some sleep or something."

"Here, drink this. It's chamomile."

Aura handed Ruth a steaming cup of tea and Ruth took a sip. The soothing warmth slipped down her throat, warming her from the inside out. Slowly, it seemed as if every muscle in her body were starting to uncoil.

"It's good, isn't it?" Terra said, sitting down across from her. "It's my special recipe."

"It's amazing," Ruth said with a smile. She leaned back, cradling the teacup in her hands.

"That's it. Just take a deep breath and relax," Aura told her. "Everything is going to be fine."

"This does feel kind of good," Ruth admitted, leaning her head back and closing her eyes. She sipped her tea, relishing the warmth. "Maybe just for a little while . . ."

"Yeah. Just for a little while," Aura said in a soothing voice.

Ruth breathed in through her nose and out through her mouth, then took another sip of tea. *Oh, yeah.* This was exactly what she needed. All the tension in her body melted away. The throbbing in her head subsided. She knew that she should be trying to figure out a way to get her memory back, to try to recall what had happened to her, but at least she knew she was home now. These girls clearly knew her. They knew what she liked to eat, they had pictures of her, they even knew she had a shoe fetish. She had to believe that she belonged here, and that her memories would come back in time.

For now, however, it just felt so good to stop. To rest. To let it all go. She was safe. That was all that mattered.

Very soon she was drifting off to sleep, happy that Aura had found her when she did and brought her back. And confident that, very soon, she would have answers to all of her questions.

"That picture was totally perfect!" Aura said as she followed Delilah back into the kitchen at the rear of the house—as far away as possible from the sleeping Phoebe Halliwell. She placed her teacup down on the countertop quietly. "I think that really convinced her, you guys. Nice work."

Delilah shrugged modestly and took a sip of her own tea. "I knew my breaking-and-entering talents would come in handy sooner or later. Those Halliwells have so many pictures of themselves, I bet they didn't even realize those shots were gone. Egomaniacs."

"Hey! What about my Photoshop abilities?" Terra asked, always looking for approval. "You guys thought my night classes were a waste of time, remember? But she didn't notice a thing."

"You're right, Terra. You did great," Aura said, squeezing the girl's shoulder. Terra beamed.

"I fed her some of the backstory we came up with too," Delilah added. "The stuff about college and when we met."

"And she didn't question any of it?" Aura asked.

"Didn't even bat an eye," Delilah said.

"This is so great! She's totally buying our

act!" Terra exclaimed, clasping her hands.

"Yeah, no thanks to your overacting," Delilah drawled, rolling her eyes. "What *was* that?"

"What?" Terra pouted. "I thought I did fine."

"'Meet us? You've known us for *years*!'" Delilah mocked, dramatically tipping her head back and touching the back of her hand to her forehead. "What are you, auditioning for *All My Children*?"

Terra crossed her arms over her chest and lowered her chin. "Well, whatever. I didn't see Phoebe complaining," she said petulantly.

"Well, the good news is, she remembers nothing," Delilah said, placing the muffin tray into the steel sink. "Girl is totally and completely ours."

"Thanks to my no-fail memory spell," Aura said, popping a bit of a cranberry muffin into her mouth.

"That was pretty brilliant," Delilah admitted. She pulled up a stool and straddled it. "Almost as good as the cloaking spell I put on the house."

"Which, by the way, she felt when she walked in," Aura told her in a scolding tone. "I think I even saw her hair stand on end."

"Hey. It's a powerful spell," Delilah shot back.

"Do you think it worked?" Terra asked, looking up at the ceiling fan as if she thought the whole house might cave in on her at any second.

"Gimme a break. We picked Phoebe up, drove

her across town, dumped her in a whole different alley, waited for Sleeping Beauty to wake herself up, and then brought her here," Delilah said. "It's been almost three hours. If her sisters could sense her, they would have busted in here by now."

"Yes. Nice work," Aura congratulated her. "Let's just hope the traveling spell we put on her works as well. Because we're going to have to leave the house with her eventually."

"They're gonna figure it out," Terra said, toying nervously with a dish towel, wrapping it around and around her hand. "I mean, they're the Charmed Ones. Sooner or later, they're going to figure a way through our magic and come for us."

"Way to be confident," Delilah said.

"No, she's right. We have to work fast," Aura told them. "But now that we have Phoebe's . . . I mean *Ruth's* powers, that shouldn't be a problem. We should be able to collect the rest of the amulets in no time."

"I still can't believe your grandmother hasn't tried to get hers back," Terra said.

Aura's face burned at the mention of her traitorous grandmother, but she shrugged it off. "Yeah, well, maybe she finally realized that the amulet belongs with me—the granddaughter with actual power—instead of with my wuss cousin, Tilly."

There was also the fact that her grandmother was old and weak and didn't have the greatest short-term memory anymore. All of which was currently working in Aura's favor.

"I just don't get it. If the coven leaders from way back when knew the amulets had so much power, why split them up among four different covens?" Delilah asked, leaning her forearms on the counter. "Wouldn't you keep them together? I mean, with that kind of power, they could have taken over the world."

Aura and her friends had pondered this question hundreds of times. As legend had it, the amulets had once been in the possession of one coven, but their power had grown to the point where the coven leaders had been unable to control it. Afraid to destroy the amulets, they decided to rend the coven into four separate parts and give each of the newly-formed covens one of the amulets, to be passed down from generation to generation to a Wicca who would keep the trinket safe—but never use its power. The moment Aura had heard this story as a child, she had known that the amulet around her grandmother's neck was destined to be hers, and she had waited patiently for the day her grandmother would finally bestow it upon her. Then, a few weeks back, when Aura had gone on one of her regular visits to her grandmother's nursing home, the old woman had told her that she intended to give the amulet to Tilly—that she was concerned about Aura's intentions.

After that, Aura had been forced to take

matters into her own hands. She'd stolen the amulet while her grandmother was sleeping and started on this quest to find the other three. A few days later, the police had shown up on Aura's doorstep asking about a family heirloom, but Aura had simply laughed them off, telling them her grandmother was *not all there*. After a few harmless questions, the cops had left her alone, and now she was free. Free to pursue her destiny.

"Well, it was their loss," Aura said blithely. "And now, it's our turn."

"Once we have all four of those amulets, we'll be invincible," Delilah said with a wicked grin. Even Terra had to smile at that one.

"And once we're *invincible*, we'll get rid of Phoebe's sisters—and then *we'll* be the most powerful witches in the world," Aura announced.

They lifted their cups and clinked them, then downed the rest of their tea.

"Nice work, by the way, naming her Ruth," Delilah said with a smirk.

"Yeah. That was just for my own personal fun," Aura replied. "Witch needed to be knocked down a few pegs. I mean, gorgeous, successful, powerful—where does she get off?"

"I'll have to make up a fake degree for her later," Delilah said.

"Oooh! And I'll embroider an *R* on that robe we got for her," Terra added. "It's all in the details."

"Perfect!" Aura said, slinging her arm over Terra's shoulders.

They all walked out into the dining room to watch their visitor doze. Phoebe let out a small snore and smiled in her sleep.

"I just can't wait to put her to work," Aura said mischievously. "Once we get *Ruth* fully on our side, her sisters won't know what hit them."

Chapter 4

Piper and Paige orbed into the living room at the manor, where they found Leo sitting on the couch in front of the TV, a sleeping Wyatt in his arms. He stood up the moment they arrived, relief flooding his face. Baby Wyatt stirred and turned his face toward his father's chest, letting out a little breath of air and a moan.

"Thank God, you're all right," Leo whispered.

"Not exactly," Piper replied.

"Why?" Leo asked, his eyes flashing with concern. He looked back and forth between the two sisters, then realized what was off. "Where's Phoebe?"

"*That* is a very good question," Paige said. "One we hope you can help us answer."

Leo glanced at Piper in confusion. She reached over and took her son from Leo's arms carefully, then walked with him to the sunroom. Paige and Leo followed. As Piper lowered Wyatt into his crib, she felt the overwhelming rush of love she felt whenever she looked at his adorable, sleeping face. At these times, when he looked so sweet and vulnerable, all she could think about was protecting him. But what kind of protector was she when she had lost her own sister?

Her heart squeezed and she stood up straight, tossing her long hair over her shoulder.

"We can't find Phoebe," she told Leo, walking past him into the dining room. She didn't want their conversation to wake Wyatt.

"What do you mean, you can't find her?" Leo asked. He toyed with his wedding ring as he stepped up to the end of the table. "When did you see her last?"

"Well, we were battling Flecter demons, and we decided to split up to take them on one-on-one," Paige told him, shoving her hands into the front pockets of her jeans. "Piper and I did our thing and then found each other, but Phoebe never came back."

"We just spent an hour searching the alleys for her, but there was no sign," Piper added.

"You don't think . . . ," Leo began, then thought the better of finishing the sentence.

"We don't know," Piper admitted, trying to ignore the depth of the fear inside her. "She definitely vanquished her demon, but we have no idea what happened to her after that."

"Can you sense her?" Paige asked, her voice

pitched up an octave in hope. "I tried, but I . . . couldn't."

Leo took a deep breath and closed his eyes. Piper watched him for any sign that he was hearing anything, any trace of recognition. All she saw on his face was concern. Finally, after what seemed like an eternity, Leo opened his eyes again.

"This is weird," he said.

"What?" Piper asked, a flicker of hope springing inside of her. At least he hadn't announced that Phoebe was completely off the radar.

"Well, I feel *something*, but it's very faint, and it's not really Phoebe," he said.

"Huh?" Paige asked, expressing exactly what was in Piper's mind.

"It's her, but it's not her," Leo said, clearly struggling to explain. "I'm not sure. I've never felt anything like this before."

"But she's alive," Piper said.

"I think so," Leo replied, looking apologetic.

"Well, where is she?" Paige asked impatiently.

"I don't know. The sensation is too weak for me to tell."

"Too weak to tell?" Piper repeated, her voice starting to take on that shrill quality she hated. That quality that meant she was starting to panic. "That doesn't sound good."

Leo didn't disagree.

"Well, maybe she's in the underworld," Paige

suggested. "Maybe one of the Flecter demons came and took her."

"No. Then I wouldn't be able to sense her at all," Leo reminded them.

"All right, that's it. To the attic," Piper said, turning around and heading for the stairs. "I'll call for her, you scry."

"Sounds like a plan," Paige said, orbing out.

Piper rolled her eyes. "Don't take me with you or anything!" she shouted after her sister. She took Leo's hand. He blinked, momentarily confused. "Well? Let's go!"

Two seconds later, Piper and Leo appeared in the attic, where Paige was already bent over a map of San Francisco. She held one of Phoebe's crystals over the map and twirled it, waiting for it to fall and reveal Phoebe's whereabouts. Piper walked over to her mortar and pestle and quickly crunched up some rosemary, cypress bark, and taro root. Then she closed her eyes and tried to reach out with her mind.

Come on, Phoebe, she thought. *Hear me.*

She took a deep breath and spoke.

Power of the witches rise,
Course unseen across the skies,
Come to Us who call you near,
Come to Us and settle here.

Then came the part she hated. She picked up a clean dagger and pricked her fingertip with it.

A drop of deep red blood appeared. Piper winced and held her finger over the mortar, letting the blood drip in.

> *Blood to blood I summon thee,*
> *Blood to blood return to me.*

She waited for that rush of warmth she got whenever this particular spell worked. Waited for some kind of movement in the air or a flash of white orbs. But there was only silence. Finally she opened her eyes again.

"Dammit," she said under her breath, seeing only Leo and Paige before her. "Anything?" she asked Paige.

The crystal was still spinning.

"Nothing," Paige said.

Piper's stomach turned. This had to be a mistake. Phoebe could not be missing after only one tiny battle with three vanquished demons. Together, the sisters had been through far worse than that and had come out on the other side just fine.

"Come on," she said, flicking her fingers at Paige. "Do this with me."

"Piper," Paige said, "I don't think it's gonna work. I mean, there's clearly something strange going on here. "

"It has to. It'll be stronger with both of us," Piper said, ignoring Paige's logic. "Now get over here."

Paige glanced at Leo, then dropped the crystal and got up. She walked over to Piper and held her hand. Already, Piper felt better. They had lost sisters before, and they had always found them somehow. This time was going to be no different.

"We're going to do this as many times as it takes," Piper said firmly. "We'll do it all night if we have to."

Paige squeezed her hand reassuringly, and together they recited the spell.

Paige awoke with a start and squinted at the sunlight pouring in through the attic windows. She lifted her head and winced. Something was stuck to her face. A thick sheet of parchment. She batted it away and sat up to look around. Apparently she had fallen asleep with her butt on the couch and her cheek resting on the Book of Shadows on the coffee table. Not good for the back or the skin.

It took Paige a moment to remember why she was in the attic instead of her own bed, and when she did, her whole body flooded with dread. She looked around and saw Piper passed out on the other end of the couch and Leo dozing in the chair. Wyatt was in his playpen near the door, quietly toying with his teddy bear. There was only one person missing.

Phoebe.

"Piper, wake up," Paige said, sitting up

straight and stretching her arms over her head. She reached down and shook Piper's leg.

"What? Phoebe?" Piper said, opening her eyes.

"She's not here, honey," Paige told her, trying to sound soothing.

Piper was fully awake in an instant and pushed herself to her feet. She looked at the stained-glass windows all around her as if they had betrayed her. "Is it morning already? How is it morning?"

"We fell asleep," Paige told her, shoving aside the blanket that was strewn over her legs.

"How could we have fallen asleep?" Piper asked shrilly. "Phoebe is missing, and we fell asleep?"

Leo roused himself and rubbed his eyes. "Piper, calm down."

"No. This is insane. We have to do something," Piper said, walking out of the room.

Paige jumped up to follow her, and together they barreled down the stairs.

"Do what?" she asked Piper.

"I'm going to call Darryl," Piper said, running her hand along the banister as she made her way to the first floor. "Maybe he can, I don't know, put out an APB or something."

"You really think that Darryl's going to find her after scrying and calling for a lost witch didn't work?" Paige asked.

"Well, I have to do *something*, Paige," Piper

shouted, whirling around at the bottom of the stairs to face her. "We can't just—"

There was a crash in the living room and Paige and Piper both turned toward the sound. Paige's jaw pretty much hit the floor at what she saw. A pair of fairies flitted about the room, chasing each other along the ceiling and around the light fixture, their wings fluttering like hummingbirds'. Half a dozen leprechauns bickered and gestured, pacing the room in their green waistcoats and plaid dresses. A giant leaned back against the wall, where a crack was forming under its weight, chatting with a translucent muse in a pink toga. Two nymphs in flowing green dresses danced around a satyr, holding garlands of flowers and giggling. There were magical creatures *everywhere*.

"What the—" Paige began.

"Oh, no. Not now," Piper said, leading the way to the living room. "What on Earth is going on in here?" she said through her teeth.

Everyone and every*thing* turned to look at her.

"I broke a vase. Sorry," one of the Seven Dwarves said, holding up the pieces. "I know an elf who can fix it. He's very good with ceramics."

"I don't care about the vase," Piper said, taking the shards from him. "What are you all doing here?"

A leprechaun with red hair and a scraggly staff stepped forward and bowed slightly.

"Teague of the Lea, at your service," he said. "I
apologize for the early arrival, but when I told
everyone of Phoebe's consent, there was quite a
clamor. Everyone wanted to be first in line, so
here we are. But a day early."

Paige looked at Piper, dumbfounded. "Do *you*
have any idea what he's talking about?" she
asked.

"Not a clue," Piper replied impatiently.

"I'm talking about Phoebe. 'Ask Phoebe?'"
Teague explained, throwing his arms wide. "She
didn't tell you?"

"Tell us what?" Paige asked, crossing her
arms over her chest.

"She offered to do a weekend counseling session for us," one of the nymphs replied, twirling
forward, her strawberry-blonde ringlets flying.
She had perfect, creamy white skin and rosy
cheeks, and her green eyes glowed with happi-
ness. "You mortals aren't the only ones who
need advice, you know. Magical beings occa-
sionally need a kind ear."

"And, boy, do we ever," a chubby blonde leprechaun woman said, stepping up next to
Teague.

"Are you kidding us with this?" Piper said.
She turned toward Paige. "What was Phoebe
thinking?"

Paige took a deep breath and stepped forward. "Listen up, everyone. I'm sorry to say that
the counseling session has been cancelled. We

apologize for any inconvenience, but you're all going to have to go now. Thank you for coming, and . . . buh-bye." There was a grumble of discontent throughout the room and Paige lifted her hands. "We're in the middle of a crisis situation right now and I'm afraid there's nothing we can do for you."

"We're not going anywhere," the giant said, his voice a loud rumble.

"Yeah!" a few of the creatures cheered.

"We were promised a service and we're not leaving here until Phoebe makes good on that promise!" Teague shouted.

"Yeah! You tell her!" the other leprechauns cheered, making tiny fists with their tiny hands.

Paige brought her own hand to her head and looked at Piper helplessly as the room grew more and more raucous. Staffs were raised in the air. A couple of felt hats were tossed. Some trolls in the corner knocked over a table. Paige and Piper were about to have a magical riot on their hands.

"Well," Paige said. "This could not get any worse."

Piper blew out a sigh as a fairy buzzed around her head. "Tell me about it."

Ruth sat at the breakfast table in her bright and modern kitchen, her stomach full of the amazing blueberry pancakes Delilah had served up for breakfast. After a long night of going through her bedroom, looking for anything that might spark a memory, she had needed the comfort food more than anything. Ruth had stared for over an hour at her college degree, but could remember nothing about the books she had read or the papers she had written to earn it. She had sifted through her books and jewelry and memorabilia from various trips she had apparently taken, but nothing had rung a bell. She had stared at the one picture of her with her blonde mother and brunette father with no spark of recognition, and when she had asked Aura if they could call her parents, Aura had broken the news that they had died in a car accident over a year before. Aside from her three friends, it seemed that Ruth was truly alone in the world.

Ruth's sleep had been restless and full of odd dreams that had woken her up every other hour. Whenever she sat up in bed, she couldn't recall anything about the dreams other than the fear they left her with. When the sun had finally risen, she had been more than happy to desert her double bed and retreat to the bathroom.

Daytime was much better than night. After taking a nice, hot shower, Ruth had smothered herself with the yummy vanilla-scented moisturizer in her bathroom. She had found a cushy blue sweat suit in the top drawer of her dresser and slipped it on, savoring the total comfort. All of this was going a long way toward helping her relax and forget her fretful night. If this morning was any indication of what her life was like, she was sure she could get used to it. She almost felt as if she were on vacation at some incredible bed and breakfast.

Enjoying the sunlight on the back of her neck as it streamed through the large windows, Ruth sipped her coffee and flipped through the *San Francisco Chronicle*. She hoped she might see something within its pages——a name, an address, a face—that would jog her memory. Anything.

Over by the refrigerator, Aura, Delilah, and Terra were having a heated, whispered debate about something, but Ruth did her best to ignore them. She didn't want to get in the middle of some argument, one that she would have no idea how to navigate anyway. Luckily, her friends hadn't tried to drag her into it. How was she supposed to know whose side to take on any given issue? It had taken her half an hour just to decide between orange juice and coffee.

Finally, Delilah broke away from the group and walked over to take Ruth's plate. This morning she wore a dark purple belly shirt and black yoga pants, but her hair was still plaited into two braids.

"How was your breakfast?" she asked with a thin smile.

"You are an incredible cook, Delilah," Ruth said, folding the newspaper. "Are you a chef?"

Delilah scoffed. "Yeah, right."

Ruth blinked as Delilah turned and walked away. Delilah seemed to run very hot and cold toward her, and Ruth had no idea why. But at least Aura and Terra were always light and smiling.

"So, Ruth, ready for our morning meditation?" Terra said, gliding over and gathering up the newspapers.

"Meditation?" Ruth asked.

"Oh, sorry. I keep forgetting that you don't remember," Terra said, biting her lip. "We do it every morning," she explained, handing the papers off to Aura, who stuffed them in a bin under the counter. "It helps us find our center and reconnect with Mother Earth. It might help you clear your mind and remember something about yourself."

"Speaking of which, what's my last name?" Ruth asked.

Terra hesitated for a split second and looked at Delilah.

"It's Miller," Delilah said. "Ruth Miller."

"Miller," Terra added with a grin.

"Miller," Ruth said slowly, letting the name roll off her tongue. It didn't sound right to her, but then, nothing did. "And what do I do for a living?" she asked.

"What do you do for a living?" Delilah asked.

"Yeah. I mean, I do have a job, right?" Ruth asked with a smile. "Something has to pay for all those fabulous clothes in my closet."

"Oh, of course," Delilah said. "It's just . . . you're sort of between jobs right now."

"I am?" Ruth asked.

"Yes. You *were* a teacher," Terra said quickly. "Of English. You know, books and writing and stuff. But now, you're . . . not."

"Why not?" Ruth asked.

"You . . . got fired," Terra blurted.

"I did?" Ruth said, her heart dropping. "Why?"

Delilah rolled her eyes and walked over to the table. "You didn't get *fired* fired," she said, rubbing the back of Terra's head like she was a little kid. "The private school you were working at closed. But don't worry. You'll find another job."

"You're *really* good at what you do," Terra said with a nod.

"Yeah?" Ruth said, feeling a bit better.

"And besides, this will give you time to get well," Delilah said. "You can concentrate on getting your memory back."

Ruth considered this and realized that Delilah was right. She had no idea what she would do if she had to go into a classroom and try to teach a lesson. She couldn't recall a single lesson she had ever taught.

"So, will you come meditate with us?" Terra asked.

Ruth lifted her shoulders and pushed her

chair back from the Formica table. "Okay. If you think it'll help."

"I definitely do!" Terra said excitedly.

Aura stepped away from the counter and took Ruth's hand, leading her into a small, sparsely decorated room off the living room. There were mats and pillows on the hardwood floor, and a few colorful wall hangings with Asian markings. In the far corner sat an old-fashioned trunk with a gold latch and lock, but otherwise the room was empty. Delilah carried in four candles and placed them in front of the mats, then lit them with a long match. The scents of lavender and vanilla instantly filled the room.

"Have a seat," Aura said, indicating the mat closest to the door.

Ruth sat down as Aura pulled the thick drapes closed, shutting out the sunlight. As the others gathered around her, Ruth watched them carefully, not wanting to do anything wrong. They each sat cross-legged with their backs straight, so Ruth did the same.

I do this every morning, she told herself, trying to believe it. *Every morning, my friends and I come into this room together and meditate.*

"Okay, everyone, let's start with some breathing," Terra said, placing her hands, palms up, on her knees. "Breathe in slowly through your nose, and then out through your mouth, expelling all toxins and negative energy into the atmosphere."

Ruth did as she was told, trying to envision anything negative within her coming out through her mouth. The visual struck her as funny, and she had to work to stifle a laugh. She placed her wrists on her knees with her palms to the ceiling, to show Terra that she was trying.

"Breathe in . . . breathe out," Terra intoned in a soothing, lulling voice. "Breathe in . . . breathe out. Forget all stresses, all concerns. Find something positive to focus on. Let every muscle in your body relax, starting with your toes and feet. . . ."

As Terra continued to give direction, Ruth focused on her voice. She closed her eyes and did everything Terra instructed. She felt her muscles loosening, her body relaxing, her breath moving in and out. It was an incredible feeling to really look within herself and *feel* her body working. What else could possibly matter but this? She was starting to see why she might enjoy doing this on a daily basis.

"Terra? Shall we pass around the amulet?" Aura asked.

Her voice was an intrusion in the stillness, and Ruth opened her eyes. She saw Aura handing a small bronze disk on a black chord to Delilah, who closed it inside her fist. Delilah took a long, deep breath and held it, then blew it out noisily. She then handed the disk to Terra, who did the same. Terra smiled as she offered the disk to Ruth.

"What is that?" Ruth asked.

She could see tiny etchings in the otherwise smooth surface of the disk. There was a small hole directly through the center.

"It's an amulet. It gives us power," Aura said gently. "Helps us find our center."

"How?" Ruth asked.

"You just hold on to it," Terra told her, placing it in Ruth's palms. The metal was cold against her warm skin. "Try to connect with it," she suggested. "Try to feel its power."

Ruth felt a bit silly as she closed the amulet inside her hand and placed her wrist on her knee again. She couldn't imagine that this small piece of metal could actually hold any kind of power, but she assumed this was something she did every day as well, and she didn't want to be rude. She closed her eyes, took a deep breath, and tried to connect.

Whatever that meant.

Suddenly, an overwhelming shock of electricity shot through Ruth's body. Her breath caught in her throat, and she gasped as every one of her muscles froze up. Out of nowhere, a scene played out in her mind. A woman in a black dress screamed and tumbled to the ground in front of her house, her dark brown hair tumbling over her face. Someone reached down and snatched her necklace from around her neck. They held it up and it glinted in the sun. An amulet—*this* amulet—on a silver chain.

Then, like a flash of lightning, the vision was

gone and the world rushed back, cold and harsh. Ruth wrenched her eyes open, gasping for breath, and unclenched her fist. The amulet tumbled out, slid down her leg, and hit the floor with a clatter. Aura, Delilah, and Terra were watching her excitedly. Almost hungrily.

"What was that?" Ruth asked, her heart racing at an insane clip. "What *was* that?"

"Did you see something?" Aura asked breathlessly, leaning forward. "What did you see?"

Ruth scrambled up, petrified, her mind reeling. *What had just happened?*

Chapter 5

"Did you have a premonition?" Aura asked, shoving herself to her feet. She stepped toward Ruth, her black eyes glowing.

Ruth instinctively stepped back. What was Aura talking about? Why did she seem to know what was going on in Ruth's mind? The air in the room was thick with the heady scents emanating from the candles, making Ruth suddenly dizzy and hot. She unzipped her sweatshirt to expose the tank top beneath and fanned at her skin with her hand.

"Of course she did. Look at her!" Delilah said with an amused smile. "She looks like she's about to pass out."

"Delilah!" Terra scolded through her teeth.

"Tell us, Ruth. What did you see?" Aura asked, softly touching Ruth's arm.

"I don't understand," Ruth said. "What was that? What's a premonition?"

Aura and Delilah exchanged a look. Then

Delilah shrugged and rolled her eyes, like *You tell her.*

"It's a special power," Aura told Ruth gently, reaching out and placing her hands firmly on Ruth's shoulders. "It means you can see the future."

Her hands were steady and sure, and they had a calming effect on Ruth. But not calming enough.

"See the future? What are you talking about?" Ruth asked, turning away. Her hands were trembling, and her body kept rushing from hot to cold to hot to cold. "That's not normal, is it? Being able to see the future?"

"No. It's not normal," Terra said, standing finally. "It's a gift. It's special. It makes *you* special. The power of the goddess is strong in you, Ruth. It always has been."

"You knew I had this . . . this *gift*?" Ruth demanded of the three women. "You knew and you didn't tell me?"

"We didn't want to freak you out," Aura explained. "We figured it was hard enough that you'd lost your memory. Wrapping your brain around this might be a bit more difficult."

"Well, you were right. It is," Ruth said harshly.

Her mind raced. She kept seeing the dark-haired woman crashing to the ground over and over again. Her temples started to throb, and she pressed her fingertips against them and closed

her eyes. How was she supposed to deal with
this? Two minutes ago, she was just a normal
person learning to meditate. Now she could see
the future?

I'm going crazy. That has to be it, Ruth thought.
I'm totally losing my mind.

"Ruth, it's okay," Aura said. "You always
embraced your gift in the past. You just have to
try to remember."

Slowly, Ruth turned around. She faced her
friends—these people she had met less than
twenty-four hours ago, the only people she
knew in the world—and swallowed her fear.

"What does this mean?" she asked.

"It means you're a powerful witch," Aura
said with a smile. "It means that you can help
people."

Witch. Powerful. Witch.

Suddenly, a memory filled Ruth's mind. A
symbol of some kind. A circle with three
entwined ellipses through its center. She tried to
hold on to it, but it was gone as quickly as it had
come. Still, there was something about this that
was familiar. Aura was right. She was meant to
help people. She *was* a witch. She knew it as certainly as she knew she was a human being. She
was a powerful witch who could see the future.
How cool was that?

"Does that mean I'm supposed to help that
woman?" she asked.

Delilah was instantly on her feet. She, Aura,

and Terra stood together, studying Ruth. Their anticipation was almost palpable.

"What woman?" Delilah demanded.

"The woman in the vision," Ruth told them, seeing it all as clear as day. "Someone had attacked her and was stealing an amulet from around her neck. An amulet just like that one," she said, pointing at the disk on the floor.

Delilah and Aura looked at one another and smiled, ever so slowly. They looked like a pair of coyotes who had just been thrown a hunk of raw meat.

"What did she look like?" Terra asked finally. "Where was she?"

"She was middle-aged, with long, dark hair," Ruth told them. "And I think she was standing outside her house." She closed her eyes and concentrated, trying to recall every last detail. Suddenly she saw the sign next to the front door. "Forty twenty-five White Street," she said. "That's where she was attacked."

"This is genius!" Delilah said cheerfully.

"What is?" Ruth asked, opening her eyes in time to see Aura shoot Delilah a look.

Delilah's smile disappeared. "Nothing. It's just a cool power, that's all."

"It definitely is. Come on. Let's go," Aura told them, quickly stooping to blow out the candles.

"Go where?" Ruth asked. Her pulse started to race. She had no idea what was going on, but everyone else was clearly excited.

"To get the amulet," Aura told her. "What you *saw* was us taking it from her."

Ruth froze as a chill skittered down her back. "What? You're going to attack that poor woman?"

"No, no, no! Ruth! You've got it all wrong!" Delilah said, walking over to her and taking both her hands. "That woman is an *evil* witch. As long as she has the amulet, she can use its power for evil. But if we take it from her, we can turn its power to good."

Ruth looked up into Delilah's eyes. Delilah smiled beatifically and Ruth realized that, somehow, her having this premonition had changed her in Delilah's eyes. Delilah respected her now. Maybe even liked her. Perhaps this was why Delilah had been so iffy with her since the amnesia. Maybe she was worried that Ruth had lost her ability to have premonitions.

"Come on," Delilah said, now grasping Ruth's hand and tugging her toward the door. "You'll see that what we're doing is all for the greater good."

The greater good.

Ruth felt another warm rush of familiarity. A comforting rush.

"Okay," she said finally. "Okay, I'll come. But maybe we should talk to her first. You know, make sure we're doing the right thing?"

"Sure. Yeah. Of course," Aura said absently. "Now let's get out of here before we lose her."

Ruth followed her friends out into the sunlit living room, her pulse racing. She was still trying to grasp the fact that she was a witch. That she had powers. Part of her was completely freaked and concerned, but an even bigger part of her was excited.

She and her friends were on a mission, and for a person who had had no idea who she was a few hours ago, a mission was an enticing thing to have.

Leo watched Piper pace back and forth in front of the Book of Shadows.

"There has to be something," she said, shoving her hands into her thick hair and holding it away from her face. "Something I'm missing."

Downstairs there was another crash—and a crumble. Piper stopped pacing and winced. "That sounded expensive."

"Why don't you ask some of the houseguests for ideas?" Leo suggested, gesturing over his shoulder at the door. "Maybe one of them will think of something we haven't."

"You mean ask the crazies who are currently tearing up our house for help?" Piper said, then laughed. "No, thanks."

They could hear Paige shouting "Hey! Get your hands off that!" down in the living room.

"Maybe if *you* go to them, they'll realize how serious the situation actually is and they'll *stop* tearing up the house," Leo suggested.

Piper looked at him and heaved a sigh. He had a point. But, somehow, the last thing she wanted to do was walk into a room full of dwarves and leprechauns and nymphs and tell them that the Charmed Ones had lost one of their own and were at a complete dead end. It just seemed a tad too pathetic. Besides, Piper had always been one for taking care of things on her own. She cleaned up her own messes.

Another crash.

"Piper! A little help!" Paige shouted up the stairs.

Piper felt like she was about to explode, which, considering that her powers were tied to her emotions, was never good. She started for the door just as the phone rang. Grabbing it on instinct, she didn't even bother to check the caller ID. Maybe it was Phoebe, or at the very least, some kind of lead.

"Hello?" she said, half desperate, half hopeful.

"Yes, this is Elyse at the *Bay Mirror*," a stressed-out voice greeted her. "I'm looking for Phoebe. She hasn't shown up for work today."

Piper bristled at Elyse's irritation. Like Phoebe's job was really at the top of their priority list right now.

"Well, I'm sorry, Elyse, but we don't exactly know where Phoebe is, so I can't help you, okay? 'Bye," Piper said.

She dropped the phone onto the couch and

started for the door again, but stopped when she saw the look on Leo's face.

"What?" she asked impatiently.

"What was that?" he asked. "Elyse is going to freak out!"

"I'm sorry! I just couldn't deal with her right now, okay? My sister is missing and there are trolls and giants and who knows what else tearing apart my ancestral home. Both of which are just a bit more important than Elyse and her little paper," Piper ranted.

The phone rang again. They both stared at it for a moment. Piper took a deep breath and picked it up. Elyse was railing in a high-pitched voice well before the line even connected.

"Elyse. Elyse!" Piper said, closing her eyes and rubbing her forehead. "Calm down."

Another crash and a bang from downstairs. Piper looked at Leo wide-eyed and gestured at him to go help Paige. As he orbed out, Piper sat down hard on the coffee table.

"I don't understand. Is Phoebe okay?" Elyse asked. "Is she really missing, because if she is, I can send over one of our investigative reporters to—"

"No!" Piper shouted. Something fell over downstairs and what sounded like a dozen billiard balls rolled across the floor. What on Earth could that have been? Whatever it was, it had upset Wyatt, who started to cry. "No. Do not send any reporters over here. Phoebe is fine.

She's just helping me with a personal crisis I'm having and she left the house for a few minutes and I overreacted. Okay? We'll send her in to work as soon as we can."

"Well, can I talk to her?" Elyse asked impatiently.

Piper's shoulders tensed. "Not just now. Like I said, she's out of the house. But I'll have her call you back as soon as she can, okay? 'Bye now!"

Piper hung up the phone, then turned it off completely. She had been forced to shout her last few sentences over Elyse's continuous rant, but she'd chosen to ignore it. The woman simply did not know how to take no for an answer.

Piper was starting to understand why her little sister had seemed so stressed lately.

"Piper!" Paige cried, sounding almost as if she was being strangled.

"You'd better get down here!" Leo added.

"Coming!" Piper shouted, shoving herself up from her seat.

The eldest witch's work was never done.

Ruth stared out the window of Delilah's SUV, her heart pounding in her fingertips, her ears, her toes. This was it. The exact house she had seen in her vision. The long driveway between huge hedges, leading up to the front door. The weathered blue shingles and white shutters. The flowering vine growing over the gate. And there it was, the sign that had brought them here—a tiny plaque in rusted iron that read 4025 WHITE STREET.

"This is crazy," Ruth said under her breath.

She really did have power. A truly awesome, weird, freaky power. Part of her had refused to believe it until that very moment.

"There she is," Delilah said, slamming the car into park. "Let's go!"

Ruth stared as a red Mini Cooper pulled into the driveway. She could see the driver behind the wheel, singing along to the radio. She didn't look like an evil witch. She looked, in fact, perfectly normal.

"Ruth! Come on!" Aura said through her teeth, opening the door for her.

"Okay, but remember—we're talking to her first!" Ruth shouted.

"Yeah, yeah," Delilah said.

Her knees quaking, Ruth stepped out of the SUV and followed after her friends as they jogged up behind the Cooper. She had no idea what was about to happen, but she had no choice but to go along. Where would she be without these girls? Wandering the streets, bleeding from the head, basically. Instead, she had a home and a name and a purpose. They were trying to show her who she was and why she was here. She couldn't exactly turn around and walk away. Not now.

The woman got out of her car and grabbed a

bag full of groceries, humming to herself the whole way. She was wearing the same black dress she'd been wearing in Ruth's premonition, and the amulet was fastened around her neck with a simple silver chain. She walked around the front of her car to the door, not noticing that she had visitors. Aura and Delilah exchanged a mischievous look. Ruth glanced at Terra and her heart dropped. Terra just looked scared.

"Look who we've finally found," Aura said, stepping forward and making herself known.

The woman dropped her bag of groceries in surprise. A few oranges rolled out and bounced along the walkway and into the grass. Her hand flew immediately to the amulet.

"You can't harm me," she said, her voice firm.

"Watch us," Delilah said, reaching for Aura's hand.

All the little hairs on Ruth's neck stood on end. Something wasn't quite right. "Hey! What happened to talking?"

Aura ignored Ruth and reached for Terra, but she never got there. Just at that instant, the woman opened her mouth and let out a blood-curdling scream—and, along with it, an incredible blast of white-hot wind that blew Ruth and all her friends right off their feet and onto the lawn behind them. Ruth's head slammed back onto the hard ground, and for a moment the whole world spun. Then, before she knew it, Aura was hauling her to her feet.

"See? What did I tell you? She's clearly evil!" Aura said, tossing her hair out of her face. "And you wanted to *talk*."

Ruth's heart was in her throat. Aura was right. With power like that, how could this woman be anything *but* evil?

"Here! Hold my hand!" Aura instructed.

The four women linked hands and stepped forward shakily. The woman was fumbling for her keys at the door. Adrenaline rushed through Ruth's veins, making her breath come short and shallow. They had to stop this evil witch. They had to take her down before she used that sick power on someone else.

"We four stand, hand in hand, forming an impenetrable band. Let their powers fuel my own. Let us all have powers grown," Aura, Terra, and Delilah recited.

Instantly, Ruth felt a powerful zing of electric energy shoot through her body. All at once, various emotions rushed in on her, and somehow she could tell that they were coming right off of her friends. She felt Aura's determination, Delilah's lust for power, and Terra's nervous resolution, all of it mixing together to form an incredibly intense cocktail of energy inside her. Ruth felt more alive than she had since waking up in that alley. More powerful. Like she could take on the world.

Aura let go of her hand and lifted her palm into the air just as the woman managed to open the door to her house. She was about to step inside to safety when, suddenly, she was lifted straight up off the ground. With a shout of surprise, she dropped her keys and kicked out her legs, which were now dangling at least ten feet from the fallen bag of groceries below.

"What the . . . ," Ruth said, her eyes wide. "Are you doing that?" she asked Aura.

"You bet your ass I am," Aura replied with a wicked grin.

"Let me down!" the woman cried, glancing around fretfully. "Let me down and I'll give you whatever you want."

"Go, Aura! Look at you!" Delilah cheered, ignoring the woman's plea.

"I knew it. I knew it would work," Aura said triumphantly.

High above, the woman opened her mouth as if to scream again.

"Delilah, do it!" Aura demanded.

Delilah pressed her palms to her temples and closed her eyes. Almost instantly, the woman's eyes closed and she went limp, her head lolling back.

"*Damn*," Delilah said, clearly impressed with herself.

Aura lowered her hand and the woman plummeted to the ground, landing with a sickening thud. Ruth rushed forward and knelt down next to the woman. She appeared to be breathing, but when she woke up, she was going to be in some serious pain from that fall.

"Why so concerned, Ruth?" Aura said, walking over. "I told you she was evil."

"I know, but . . . Sorry. I've just never seen
anything like this before," Ruth said, looking up
at her friends. "I don't think."

"Well, be happy. We just conquered an evil
witch!" Delilah said, quickly sliding her hand
over Aura's. They both laughed, giddy with
power. "You should get used to it, because we're
going to be doing a lot more of it."

"Wow. I've never seen you lift anything more
than a few inches," Terra said, looking at Aura in
awe. "And you! How did you do that, Delilah? I
thought you could only *read* thoughts."

"You can read thoughts?" Ruth asked.

"Sometimes," Delilah said with a shrug. "But
I always knew that if I could augment my
powers, I would be able to manipulate people's
minds. I just reached out and concentrated on
putting her to sleep. That was it."

"When we recited that spell, it made us all
stronger," Aura said as Ruth stood up. "We've
done it before, the four of us."

"We have?" Ruth asked, wishing she could
remember. This seemed like the kind of thing no
one would forget.

"Yeah, but never with results like that," Terra
told her. "We must all be getting closer to our
craft."

"It's amazing," Delilah said, looking at Ruth.

"I was worried that, with your amnesia, it might not work at all, but you must really be embracing the news that you're a witch."

"It felt incredible," Ruth admitted with a smile. "I felt so connected to all of you."

"Cool, isn't it?" Delilah said.

"Definitely," Ruth replied.

Terra stood up and crossed her arms over her chest. "But I didn't get to use *my* power."

Aura rolled her eyes. "Go ahead and do it."

"What's the point now? We've got the amulet, and I didn't have to do anything," Terra whined.

"Come on, Terra," Delilah prodded. "You know you want to."

Finally, Terra smiled, and then she disappeared before Ruth's eyes. Just like that. One second she was there, the next second she was not.

"Where did she go?" Ruth asked.

"I'm right here," Terra's disembodied voice said. She magically reappeared between Delilah and Aura.

"Wow. Wicked power," Ruth said, impressed.

"I know," Terra replied with a blithe shrug. "Invisibility rules."

Ruth smiled in return. She looked around at the now quiet yard, which, luckily, was shielded from the neighbors' by the thick hedge. "So, what do we do now?"

"We get what we came for." Aura crouched down and snapped the amulet from the woman's neck. She spun the chain around her fingers and clasped it in her palm. "Let's hit the road."

As the foursome made their way back to the waiting SUV, Aura slipped her arm around Ruth's shoulders and gave her a squeeze.

"We did a good thing here. Now she won't be able to use the amulet's powers for evil anymore. It's safe with us," Aura said, her voice full of pride. She handed the amulet to Ruth, and it glinted in the sun. "How does it feel?"

Slowly, Ruth smiled. "It feels good. Really good."

Chapter 6

Aura, Delilah, and Terra chatted cheerfully as they walked back into the house and through the living room. They sounded like a bunch of teenage girls returning from a successful trip to the mall. Ruth smiled as she trailed behind them, lost in her own thoughts. She felt lucky. Lucky and serene and at peace.

"You look happy," Aura said, twirling around to walk backward as they entered the meditation space.

"I am," Ruth said, surprised at the thought. "I can't believe what we just did."

"Incredible, isn't it?" Terra asked, grasping both of Ruth's arms. "Don't you just feel so full of life?"

"I do, actually," Ruth said. "I feel like I could do anything."

"That's what being a witch is all about," Aura told her. "You have the power to take on the world."

She paused in front of a wooden wall cabinet that Ruth hadn't noticed before. It was shallow, with two solid doors and a small iron lock. Aura pulled out a chain that was tucked under her T-shirt and used the key that dangled from it to open the lock. Inside were four small hooks lined up in a row. The original amulet hung on the first hook—Aura must have placed it there before the girls had left. Now Aura held her hand out to Ruth.

"The amulet?" she asked.

Ruth stepped forward and handed over the trinket. She felt almost sad to part with it. The amulet was like a trophy, representing their good deed. But she was sure that if Aura was locking the amulets up, she had a good reason.

"What are the other hooks for?" Ruth asked.

"The other amulets," Aura replied. "Once we find them."

"There are four amulets in all," Delilah explained, hooking her thumbs into the waist-band of her yoga pants. "Eventually, we're going to retrieve all of them and reunite them here. With us."

"Where they will be used for good," Terra added rather loudly.

"We don't know where they are?" Ruth asked.

"No. That's why you're here," Terra said with a shrug and a smile.

Aura shot Terra a look of death and Delilah

sighed, rolling her eyes and leaning back against the wall.

"What she means is, we've always hoped that the blessing of your power might help us find the amulets. In fact, it was a premonition of yours that found us the first one," Aura told Ruth.

"Really? Where did it come from?" Ruth asked.

"This elderly witch in a nursing home was holding on to it," Delilah told her, shrugging a shoulder. "It was relatively easy to get it. She didn't have much fight left in her."

"No. She definitely didn't," Aura agreed. "Getting the other two amulets might prove to be a bit more difficult." She reached for Ruth's hand. "But don't worry about it. For now, we can relax."

Her fingers clasped Ruth's and, immediately, Ruth was hit with another vision. She gasped and her eyes closed as a horrible scene played itself out before her eyes. The four of them were inside some strange, old-fashioned house, and two witches were attacking them. The witches both had dark hair and one of them incinerated Aura with a mere flick of her hand. Aura screamed in horror as she met her grizzly demise. Then the other witch jumped out from her hiding place and stood behind Delilah. The witch pulled her arm back, exposing a tiny bottle glint in her hand before she tossed it at Delilah. Ruth heard another blood-curdling scream, and Delilah was engulfed in flames.

Then, suddenly, the scene was gone. Ruth opened her eyes and found herself kneeling on the floor, her hand still clasped in Aura's.

"Are you all right?" Terra asked, crouching in front of her. "You must have seen something horrible!"

Ruth gasped for breath, feeling as if her heart were being wrenched out of her chest. Seeing her friends die like that was almost more than she could take. Why would those witches want to hurt them like that? Who knew there was so much evil in the world?

"What did you see?" Aura asked, kneeling as well. Her dark eyes were full of concern. Ruth could hardly look at her, knowing that she was going to die. How horribly she was going to die.

"Witches," she managed to blurt out. "Evil witches. And they killed you," she said, looking from Aura to Delilah, who had finally pushed herself away from the wall. "Both of you."

"What did they look like?" Delilah asked grimly. "Did they have the amulets?"

"No. I don't think so. At least, I didn't see any. One of them had dark, almost black hair, about shoulder length. Thick lips. Sort of a wicked look about her," Ruth explained. "The other had long brown hair and was more of a no-nonsense type. She . . . she killed you with a flick of her wrist," she said, staring at Aura. "And her eyes were so cold. Like she was completely focused on what she was doing."

Ruth covered her face with her hands and shuddered. This couldn't happen. She couldn't let her only friends in the world die. What would she do without them?

"We know who they are," Aura said, her voice serious. "They're very powerful witches, and it sounds as if they're coming for us."

"What are we going to do?" Ruth asked, near tears.

Aura placed her hand on Ruth's back and rubbed up and down. "It's okay. It's going to be okay."

"How, exactly?" Delilah spat. "If she already *saw* it—"

"Then we just have to change it," Aura said firmly. "The future is changed with every choice we make. I think this was a warning."

"A warning?" Ruth asked.

"Yes. To keep us going," Aura said, standing. She helped Ruth to her feet. "We have to find the last two amulets before these witches attack. Once we have all four, we'll be unstoppable. They won't be able to do the things you saw them do to us."

"They won't?" Terra asked tremulously.

"No, they won't," Aura told her. "Now, where did you see this battle taking place? Were we here in our house?"

Slowly, Ruth shook her head. "No. Not here.

We were in some old house. Lots of antiques and chintz and flowers."

Delilah snorted. "Sounds totally cheesy."

Ruth smirked, happy that the girls didn't seem as freaked out as she was.

"Good. Well, then, if we don't leave the house for a little while, then it can't come true," Aura told them all. "We're still safe here. So let's all just relax, and then we'll figure out what we're going to do next."

"Sounds like a plan," Delilah said.

"I'm in," Terra added.

"Me, too," Ruth said, her blood pressure finally starting to return to normal.

Aura locked up the cabinet holding the amulets and turned to lead her friends out of the room. Ruth followed last. As she closed the door behind her, she looked across the cozy meditation space. She just hoped that Aura was right, that they were safe within these walls. Because she did not want to see her friends die like that in real life. She would do anything to keep it from happening.

Piper lifted her fingers to her mouth and whistled as loudly and shrilly as humanly possible. Instantly, all the chaos in the living room came to a halt. Everyone froze, without even the help of her time-freezing power. Piper took in the scene and sighed. The curtains had been torn from their rods, which hung at precarious angles. Several windows had

been broken, and there were shards of glass
and ceramic all over the floor. The TV was toast.
Clearly having been hit by some power or
another, it was smoking, and the screen had been
burnt out. The only piece of furniture still
standing was the couch. Everything else was
either completely destroyed or on its way.

Of course, the most disturbing sight was
Paige hovering upside down in the center of the
room, her hair and arms dangling, as a group of
fairies held her aloft. And then there was Leo,
who had been cornered by the giant and was
staring up at the goon as though his life were
flashing before his eyes.

"Let my family go, please," Piper said.

The fairies quickly turned Paige upright
and placed her gently on the ground. With
a grunt, the giant slowly backed away from
Leo, staring him down the whole way.
Relieved, Leo made his way over to Piper, never
taking his eyes off the huge ogre. He was so
distracted, he tripped on a piece of broken table
and fell against Piper's side. She held out
her arms to steady him, and he laughed nervously.

"Everyone all right?" Piper asked through
her teeth as Paige joined them.

"It's gonna take about a year for all the blood
to rush back out of my head, but, otherwise,
sure. I'm fine," Paige said, holding her fingers to
her temple.

"I'm all right," Leo told her. "Ego bruised, though."

"Don't worry, honey. You could totally take him," Piper said under her breath.

Leo smiled, but the giant chuckled. Piper decided it was time to move on.

"Listen up, everyone," she said, addressing the room. "Now, I am *very* sorry, but Phoebe is not here. And it doesn't look like she's going to be here anytime soon."

The magical creatures started to grumble and Piper held up her hands.

"I know she promised all of you that she would help out, but something has happened to her, and, unfortunately, we have no idea where she is," Piper told them, swallowing her pride. "Since there is nothing the three of us can do to help you all, I'd like to kindly ask you to leave so that we can concentrate on finding our sister."

She gestured with her arms for all of them to go, but no one moved. They all simply stared at her. Dozens of pairs of magical eyes.

"Why aren't they going?" Piper asked Paige quietly.

"Possibly because we don't believe you," Teague said, stepping forward.

Piper's mouth dropped open. "Excuse me? You don't believe me?"

"One a' you Charmed Ones is always going missing or going bad or going batty," Teague said, waving his staff around.

"Excuse me? Batty?" Paige said, crossing her arms over her chest.

"You *were* the one who turned into a vampire bat, remember?" Leo said under his breath.

Paige rolled her eyes. "You say that like it was my fault."

"You're not getting outta this so easily," Teague continued. "We came here for advice, and we're not leaving until we get it!"

"Yeah!" the other creatures cheered.

Piper hung her head. Didn't they get that she was in the middle of a huge crisis here? When did the magical community become so utterly selfish?

"All right!" she said finally, wanting nothing more than to silence them. "Hold on just one second. We need to talk." She turned around and led her bemused husband and sister into the next room. "Nobody break anything!" she said over her shoulder.

"What're we going to do?" Leo asked.

"Well, I think that someone needs to start this whole counseling session," Piper said, looking at Paige. "Otherwise, they'll never leave us alone. So, Miss Paige? What do you say?"

Paige's eyes widened. "Me? Why me?"

"Well, you used to be a social worker," Piper pointed out. "You already know how to do this."

"Yeah, maybe for mortals, but that group in there is way beyond my talents," Paige said. "Besides, I think I might have an idea of how to find Phoebe."

"You do?" Piper asked hopefully.

"Yeah. I remembered something I read in one of the spell books once, and I think there might be a way to strengthen the spell to call a lost witch," Paige said. "But we don't have the supplies we need here."

"Great. So you tell me what we need and Leo and I will go shopping, and you can stay here and start counseling," Piper said.

"Hello? We're waiting!" Teague called, sticking his head out of the living room. Piper's shoulders tensed up so quickly, they rose to her ears.

"Uh, that's okay. I already know what I need and where to get it. By the time I explain it to you, I could have been there and back," Paige said quickly. "So, see ya!"

"Don't you dare!" Piper snapped.

But it was too late. With a quick twiddle of her fingers, Paige had already disappeared in a swirl of white orbs, leaving Piper and Leo alone to deal with the disgruntled magical mental patients.

Ruth sat at the dining table in the long living room, inhaling the incredible scents all around her. Terra placed a basket of warm rolls on the table, then tucked her skirt under her to sit down next to Ruth. Delilah, meanwhile, carved the roasted chicken, setting slices on each of their plates. Over in the corner, Aura fiddled with the stereo until soft guitar music filled the room. Candles flickered on the table and in the chandelier overhead. The whole scene was cozy and serene. It felt absolutely perfect. It felt like home.

But, for some reason, Ruth could not fully relax. Possibly because she couldn't seem to stop thinking about the horrible premonition she had seen earlier that day. She couldn't stop replaying Aura's and Delilah's deaths over and over again. How could they possibly be so calm, so collected, knowing what was to come? She had a feeling that if they had actually seen what she had seen, they would never have been able to sit down to a leisurely meal.

"Well, everyone . . . dig in!" Aura said as she joined them at the table.

"It all looks incredible, Delilah," Ruth said, spooning some gravy onto her meat. She wasn't at all certain that she was going to be able to eat, but she thought she should put forth the effort. After all the trouble Delilah had gone to, it would have been rude not to try.

"Thanks. It's my favorite," Delilah said, tucking in. "I figured that if it might be my last meal . . ."

Ruth's heart twisted and Terra slowly lowered her fork.

"What? I have to be able to joke about it," Delilah said.

"Let's just try to have a nice, peaceful meal," Aura said calmly. "Once we're done eating, maybe Ruth can try to get another premonition, and then we can go after the third amulet."

"Why don't I try right now?" Ruth asked.

"Because you need to relax," Aura told her, taking a bite of her potatoes. "You only got that first premonition this morning because we were meditating."

"And because I touched the amulet," Ruth reminded her. "Maybe if I held the second one and tried to concentrate—"

"You really want to do this right now?" Aura said. "Ruth, I don't want you to feel pressured."

"I don't," Ruth said honestly. What she felt was scared. Scared and determined to make sure that the vision she had experienced would never come true. "And to tell you the truth, I don't much feel like eating. As amazing as it looks."

"I understand the feeling," Delilah said. "Come on, Aura. Let's just do this."

Everyone looked at Aura. "All right. If you insist."

She pulled the key out of the collar of her dress and lifted the chain over her head. She handed the key to Terra, who jumped up and ran for the meditation room.

"You're sure you're up to this?" Aura asked Ruth, resting her wrists on the edge of the table. "It's been a trying day."

"I'm sure," Ruth replied. "I just want to get this over with."

Moments later, Terra returned with the second

amulet and handed it to Ruth as she sat down. Aura and Delilah watched over the flickering light of the candles as Ruth took the amulet into her hand. She closed her eyes and blocked out everything but the cool metal against her skin— no music, no scents of the food, no feeling of their eyes upon her. There was nothing but the amulet. Nothing but the amulet and its power.

Come on, Ruth thought. *Show me. Show me where the third amulet is. . . .*

Her entire body froze, and she sucked in air. She felt almost triumphant as the premonition overcame her. As clearly as a film projected on a screen, the scene played before her mind's eye. A young woman with a baby face and soft, blonde curls walking out the back door of a shop, clutching a bag of garbage. The door was clearly marked WAYS OF THE WICCA. The woman closed the door behind her and turned around. As she did, the amulet was clearly visible, dangling from a beaded necklace around her throat.

The vision disappeared and Ruth opened her eyes. The return to the now was just as dizzying and disturbing as it had been before. She waited for the feeling of disorientation to pass, then looked around the table at her friends. They gazed back at her hopefully.

"I saw it," she announced breathlessly. "I know where the third amulet is."

"Is it protecting another witch?" Aura asked.

"Yes, but she doesn't look that powerful," Ruth said. "Nothing like the last one."

Ruth couldn't imagine a woman with a cherub face like that, harnessing the type of evil power the first witch had had. She seemed too young and innocent. Maybe even clueless.

But she's evil, don't forget that, she told herself. *You almost let the last woman trick you.*

"Is she nearby?" Delilah asked.

Ruth's brow knit. "I'm not sure. She was coming out the back door of this shop called WAYS OF THE WICCA." She looked around at the others. "Ring any bells?"

"I know it," Terra said quietly, toying with her napkin. "It's downtown. I buy a lot of my incense there."

"Great. You can navigate," Aura said, pushing herself away from the table with a determined smile. A smile that made Ruth's heart start to pound with anticipation. "Come on, ladies," Aura said. "Let's do our thing."

Chapter 7

Paige stood in line at the counter of her favorite herbal and magic shop as Nayla Braun, the young proprietor, rang up a large order for the couple in front of her. Dozens of glass and bronze talismans hung from the ceiling, dancing each time the door opened and let in the cool breeze. Baskets of herbs and flowers and roots and weeds were set up in rows down the center of the store, filling the place with a sweetly pungent mélange of scents. All along the outer walls were shelves overflowing with good luck charms, crystal balls, chalices, and cauldrons, along with tons of other mystical paraphernalia. Normally, Paige could spend an hour browsing along the shelves, checking out the merchandise and getting inspiration for new potions, but today she had no such luxury.

The longer Phoebe was out there missing, the smaller the chances that she'd be found. Paige had watched enough crime dramas in her day to know that.

She glanced at the items in her wicker basket to check that she had grabbed all the necessary ingredients. A few stalks tied up with twine, some herbs that she had measured out into paper bags. She had to make sure she hadn't forgotten anything. Phoebe's life might depend on this spell.

Okay. Pennyroyal . . . check, foxglove . . . check, fresh tarot root . . . check.

She took a deep breath and glanced at her watch. Phoebe had been missing for almost twenty-four hours. Twenty-four hours with no sign of her, no clues whatsoever, no real course of action to follow. Every other time one of her sisters had gone AWOL—and there had been a few—there had always been at least some sort of lead to go on, something to work toward. But this was completely different. No threat. No ransom. No demon to blame it on or spell to reverse. She was just gone.

And it's all my fault, Paige thought, her heart twisting into a tight ball. *I should never have assumed that the Flecter demon was just some lower-level demon. Never should have tried to kill him off with that measly potion. I should have done my homework. If I had, I could have offed the first Flecter myself, and the whole tribe never would have been there to attack us. And Phoebe never would have run off by herself. Instead of being missing right now, she'd be at home, counseling Teague and his band of magical misfits.*

Paige sighed at the thought. She could only imagine what was going on at the manor just then—how much Piper was hating her for bailing. But she *had* to come here to get these ingredients. This whole Phoebe thing was her fault, and *she* had to fix it.

"Hi again," Nayla said cheerily as Paige stepped up to the tall counter and placed her basket next to the cash register. Nayla's blue eyes sparkled and her rosy cheeks glowed under the soft lights. "You've been coming in a lot recently."

Paige shrugged and forced a smile. "Going through a trial-and-error period," she improvised. "A lot of my potions have gone awry."

The truth was, most of Nayla's customers probably didn't need as many supplies as Paige and her sisters did. They weren't out there fighting demons every day of the week.

Or searching for lost sisters . . .

Nayla smiled sympathetically and started to ring up Paige's purchases. "Well, if you're going to be using all of this, then I bet your next one will be seriously powerful," she said, eyeing the huge amounts of herbs.

"That's the idea," Paige said under her breath.

"That'll be twenty-five dollars and thirteen cents," Nayla said as the receipt popped up out of the machine.

Paige paid with cash and Nayla placed everything in Paige's reusable knit bag. "Thanks," Paige said as she turned to leave.

"Good luck with your potion. And come back again!" Nayla trilled with a wave.

"I will!"

As Paige turned to leave and find someplace safe and secluded to orb from, Nayla bent down and gathered up a garbage bag in her hands, then headed for the back door. On her way out the front, Paige's knit bag slipped from her shoulder and knocked into a metal vase full of incense sticks. The vase crashed to the floor and the sticks went flying everywhere. Paige's shoulders slumped as she looked at the mess.

"Just great," she said.

She peered around the empty shop and, finding the coast was clear, was about to use her power to just orb away the mess, but then an older man walked in and started to browse around. Paige clucked her tongue and dropped to the floor to gather up the sticks. *Unbelievable.* Why was she only klutzy when she had ten more important things to do?

When she was done, Paige glanced at the browser, then at the counter. Nayla hadn't returned. It probably wasn't the best idea to leave some random guy alone in the shop, but that wasn't Paige's responsibility. On a normal day, she might have been the Good Samaritan and kept an eye on things until Nayla got back, but today, she had to get home. She picked up

her bag, turned around, and pushed the front
door open.

As soon as she stepped outside, Paige heard a
shout and a crash from the alleyway. On instinct,
she ran to the corner of the building, ready and
willing to take on the bad guys. Her heart
caught in her throat at the sight of Nayla, the
storekeeper, on her back, unconscious, her limbs
splayed out at unnatural angles. Four women
stood a bit farther down the alley, their heads
bent together, their backs to Paige.

"Oh, my God! Nayla!" Paige said, dropping
down next to her. "Nayla, are you all right?"

Nayla blinked a few times and roused herself.
Paige placed her free arm around the woman's
shoulders to help her up. As she did, she realized she had caught the attention of the four
women. Slowly, they turned to face her. Their
menacing stance sent a chill down Paige's spine.

"Can you stand?" she asked Nayla.

Nayla nodded as she steadied herself. "What
happened?"

"I'll explain later," Paige said. "For now,
you'd better just get inside."

Nayla didn't have to be told twice. She
quickly opened the back door of her shop and
slipped away.

Paige turned to face the four women. One
badass-looking girl with long, dark hair. One
pretty girl with serious evil in her eyes and some
kind of necklace dangling from her fingers. One

skittish girl who was only faking the bravado she had on.

I can take these chicks, no problem, Paige thought, preparing to do battle.

Then, finally, the fourth woman turned around, and Paige stopped breathing. She felt completely shocked and completely elated at the same time, all the blood rushing to her face.

"Phoebe!" she exclaimed.

Phoebe narrowed her eyes. "*You!*" she growled.

Ruth had never felt so much rage before in her life. At least, she *thought* she hadn't. It wasn't as if she could remember that far back. But she knew she had felt nothing like it in recent memory. The moment she turned around and saw the raven-haired witch from her vision stepping toward her, it was as if the entire world turned red. There was no way she was going to let this evil witch hurt her or her friends.

"Phoebe! Are you okay?" the girl shouted, rushing forward.

"Get her!" Aura cried.

Ruth's hands curled into fists. All she could see was the girl coming at her. She raced forward and launched herself into the air, grabbing the bottom rung on a fire escape overhead and swinging forward. She slammed the stunned witch in the chest with both feet, and the girl staggered backward and fell. Her bag of Wicca supplies flew from her grasp, its contents scattering across the alley. Evil roots and weeds, no doubt.

"Get up. Get up and fight me, witch," Ruth said, standing over the girl.

She lifted her arms instinctively and stepped back into a fighting stance. A rush of adrenaline coursed through her veins as she realized how easily and naturally this came to her. Apparently, she was some kind of experienced fighter. Who knew?

The girl coughed and pushed herself up on shaky arms. She whipped her hair over her shoulder and stared up at Ruth. Her lip was cut and blood trickled down her chin onto her blouse.

"What are you doing?" she said, wiping the blood away with the back of her hand.

"Making sure you can't hurt us," Ruth said, as Aura, Delilah, and Terra jogged over to back her up. "Now, are you going to get up and fight, or are you some kind of coward?"

"Phoebe, it's me. Paige. Your sister?" the girl said, wisely staying on the ground.

Ruth scoffed. "Yeah, right. Nice try. You're *evil*. What is this, some kind of evil-witch mind game?"

Behind her, the other girls snickered in delight. The girl on the ground looked around at them warily, clearly realizing how very outmatched she was.

"I'm not the one playing mind games," the girl—Paige—muttered.

Ruth glanced over her shoulder, then took a step back and linked hands with her friends. "What do you say we finish this? Right now."

Aura and Delilah smiled wickedly at one another. Ruth felt the power of her friends, of their connection, rush through her veins as they clasped her fingers.

"What are you doing?" Paige asked, scrambling to her feet. "Phoebe! You have to listen to me! They've brainwashed you or something!"

Ruth stared back at her. She would not let this evil witch's games affect her. She had already seen what the witch was capable of. Had heard Delilah's screams as the witch murdered her. This girl was the worst of the wicked, and she was going down.

"We four stand, hand in hand, forming an impenetrable band," Ruth recited with her friends. A hot wind kicked up, swirling around them, sending garbage and debris flying, and tossing Ruth's hair all over the place. "Let their powers fuel my own. Let us all have powers grown."

Paige's eyes narrowed as her hair whipped at her cheeks. "Well. This can't be good," she said.

Then Aura let go of Ruth's hand and raised her own. Paige flew into the air with a shout of surprise, her legs flailing beneath her.

"What are you doing?" Paige shouted. "Phoebe! You can't let them do this!"

"Aw! Look at the poor witch," Aura chided. "All helpless."

"We'll see who's helpless." Paige shot Aura a look of death. "Garbage can!" she shouted, flicking her wrist.

Suddenly, one of the metal receptacles at the back of the alley disappeared in a swirl of white light, then reappeared, spinning end over end through the air. Before Ruth could even call out a warning, the can had slammed into Aura's back and sent her flying forward. Her head smacked against the asphalt and she was knocked out cold.

"Aura!" Terra shouted, dropping to the ground.

Now that Aura's power had been extinguished, Paige began plummeting downward, but before she could hit the ground, she, too, disappeared in a swirl of light, then reappeared standing safely on the ground, right in front of Ruth and her friends. Ruth had never seen anything like it. This girl had some serious power.

"How dare you!" Delilah said, stepping forward.

"Phoebe! Come on," Paige said, reaching for Ruth's hand.

Ruth pulled free and backhanded the girl across the face. "Don't touch me!" she yelled.

Trembling, the witch brought her fingers to her cheek, tears springing to her eyes. She looked at Ruth as if betrayed.

"You'll pay for this," Delilah said, raising her hands to her head.

But before Delilah could work her magic,

Paige stood up straight, and with one last, disappointed glare, disappeared in a swirl of white light. Just like that. She was gone.

"Dammit," Delilah said, dropping her hands.

"Where did she go?" Ruth asked, stunned.

"Who knows?" Delilah said.

"You guys! She's awake," Terra announced.

Aura lifted her head from the ground and shook it, moving her jaw around as she sat up. She felt a scrape on her cheek and arched her back, making sure she was still in one piece.

"Are you okay?" Ruth asked her, kneeling next to Terra.

"That witch does not play fair," Aura said through her teeth.

"Yeah, you're okay," Terra said.

Aura picked up the fallen amulet and clasped it in her hand. "Help me up?" she asked.

Terra and Ruth grasped her under her arms, and together they struggled to their feet. Aura brushed herself off and took a deep breath.

"Where is she?" Aura asked.

"She got away," Ruth admitted.

"You know, I could have finished her off right away if you didn't always feel the need to perform your theatrics," Delilah told Aura.

"What? I wanted to show her how much power we have! You know, put a little fear into her," Aura replied.

"And that worked so well," Delilah said sarcastically.

"But where did she go?" Ruth asked, glancing around the alley. "Can she turn invisible like Terra? What's with all the crazy white light?"

"Oh . . . uh . . . we've seen that power before," Aura told her. "She can transport herself from place to place that way."

"Wow. Then she *is* a really powerful witch," Ruth said. "How are we ever going to take down someone who can just vanish at will?"

"It's a good question," Aura said, slipping her arm around Ruth's shoulders. She held up the newest addition to their amulet collection and let it dangle in front of Ruth's face. "And with this, we're one step closer to having the answer."

"I come home from a long day of guarding the gold and all I want to do is put my feet up and enjoy a pint of ale," Brian the leprechaun explained. He and his wife Gail, both of them fair-haired and chubby, with candy-apple-red cheeks, sat on the couch in the center of the living room, while the rest of the magical beings hovered along the walls and windows, talking in low tones. "But does she care about that? No! She wants me to watch the young'uns while she goes off to her dance practice." Brian huffed and yanked up the waistband of his shorts, his hairy legs dangling a foot above the floor. "It's like she doesn't realize how important my work is."

Leo and Piper exchanged a look as Gail sniffled and gazed down at the shamrock-lined handkerchief in her hands. Talk about an old-fashioned take on things. Piper felt like wringing the little guy's neck. She couldn't believe she was being forced to listen to this crap when she could have been upstairs with the Book of Shadows trying to figure out a way to find Phoebe.

"Well, what about raising your children?" Leo asked gently, leaning forward on the couch. "Isn't that important work as well?"

Piper smiled. Oh, how she loved her enlightened husband.

"A' course! But that's *her* work, not mine!" Brian said.

"That's it! Listen to me, Mr. Tiny," Piper snapped, standing up.

All the leprechauns in the room gasped.

"Oh, like it's a big shock to you all!" Piper said, glaring at them. "You're small. Get over it!" She knew she was being rude, but she couldn't help it. That's how very on-edge she was.

"Piper," Leo said in a warning tone.

"No. I'm not going to calm down," Piper said. "I can't listen to this anymore. Gail, if you want to have a life, go out and have a life. You don't need this unenlightened, craggly-faced loser holding you back."

Gail stifled a laugh behind her handkerchief and Piper smirked.

"Oh, and I suppose your husband gladly watches your baby all the time while you're off gallivanting about!" Brian shouted, shoving

himself off the couch. His booted feet landed
with a thud on the floor.

"First of all, I do not gallivant," Piper said.
She sat down again and took Leo's hand. "But,
yes, if you must know, he does help around here.
A lot. And he loves spending time with his son."

Brian looked at Leo with one eyebrow raised
in doubt. Leo shrugged apologetically. "She's
right. I love being with Wyatt. They grow up so
fast, Brian. I don't want to miss a thing."

For a split second, Brian's face changed. It
looked as if he were about to cave. But then, out
of nowhere, his surly demeanor returned.

"Of course you'd be all touchy-feely," he said
with a scoff. "You're a Whitelighter. Everybody
knows you're a buncha girly-men."

"Hey!" Leo said.

"Okay! That's it! Next!" Piper shouted, standing up again.

"But you didn't tell her to quit dancing!"
Brian exclaimed.

"And I'm not going to," Piper told him, shoo-
ing them both out. "Who's next?"

The two nymphs and the satyr danced over
and took their places on the couch. The satyr, in
his dark coat and pants, sat in the center, while
the two nymphs curled themselves around him.
One caressed his cheek with a long satin
scarf while the other toyed with his hair. The
satyr sat back and smiled, clearly loving every
minute of it.

"Okay. What's your problem?" Piper asked impatiently, sitting down next to Leo.

"We're both in love with him," one of the nymphs explained.

"We've told him to choose, but he won't," the other said as she ran her hand over his knee.

The satyr's grin widened.

"Gee, I wonder why," Piper said through her teeth.

She felt like blowing something up, just to relieve the tension, but she had a feeling that the other creatures wouldn't appreciate that.

Why can't I just have something to smash? Piper thought desperately.

At that moment, a Flecter demon with a yellow beard shimmered in right behind the couch.

"Look out!" Leo shouted, tackling Piper to the ground.

An energy ball whizzed over their heads and exploded against the wall behind them. Instantly, all the magical creatures scattered, taking cover as two more Flecters appeared in the center of the room.

Be careful what you wish for, Piper thought wryly.

"What's this? Some kind of convention?" one of the Flecters exclaimed with a laugh. "Good! Even more carnage than we were expecting."

"Run!" Piper shouted.

Pushing herself up from the floor, she slammed the first Flecter with her power, then

the second and third in quick concession, giving
herself and Leo enough time to hightail it out of
the room. They ran into the dining room, ducking out of sight on either side of the entryway.

"What do we do?" Leo asked her.

"I don't know. I haven't had time to research
them," Piper told him. "We've been concentrating on Phoebe."

Piper could hear a battle spark up between the
Flecters and the other magical creatures in the
living room. For the first time all day she was glad
to have them all there. Maybe together they'd be
able to fight these persistent buggers off.

"You should get Wyatt out of here," Piper
told Leo. "I can handle this."

"You're sure?" Leo asked.

"Yes. Just go," Piper told him.

Leo orbed out to the nursery and Piper
leaned back against the dining table. She waited.

"Come out, come out, wherever you are!" one
of the Flecters taunted, making his way across
the foyer.

At that moment, Paige orbed in, right in the
middle of the doorway.

"Hey! You're never going to believe—"

"Duck!" Piper shouted at her.

Paige turned and her eyes widened as an
energy ball came right at her. She orbed out just
in time, and the ball took out the floral center-
piece on the table. When she orbed back in, she
was directly behind Piper.

"What's going on?" she asked.

"Guess the Flecter demons weren't done with us yet," Piper said.

She peeked out of the doorway and slammed the demon with her power. "That's twice," she said, as another energy ball flew by.

"Well, this might not be the best time to discuss it, but I found Phoebe," Paige said, ducking another shot of fire.

"What? Where? Where is she?" Piper asked, relief flooding through her.

Distracted by Paige's news, she didn't see the energy ball headed toward her. It grazed her arm, throwing her back against the wall. The pain was excruciating, as if someone had just set fire to her skin. She sank to the floor, clutching her elbow, and Paige dropped down next to her.

"Are you all right?" she asked.

"It's just a scratch," Piper said, holding her breath.

"Enough of this," Paige said, standing.

The demon saw her and grinned toothily, forming another energy ball above his upturned hand. Paige lifted her own hand and grinned back at him.

"Energy ball!" she shouted.

The second it appeared above her palm, she pulled back her arm and thrust it right at the demon. The Flecter's yellow eyes widened as he saw his own power turned against him.

He exploded in a ball of red flame as the battle continued to rage behind him.

"What can I do?" Paige asked, helping Piper to her feet.

"You can tell me where Phoebe is," Piper said. She lifted her trembling fingers from her wound. They were covered in blood. "Wait . . . if you found her, why didn't you bring her back here?"

A scream of fear could be heard coming from the living room, followed by another explosion.

"We could use her right about now," Piper added.

"Yeah, well, that's the thing," Paige said. "I don't think she'd be interested in helping us."

"What do you mean?" Piper asked, a whole new wave of trepidation rushing down her spine.

"Piper, Phoebe attacked me," Paige said.

Piper's heart dropped. "She what?"

"It was like she thought I was evil," Paige said solemnly. "It was like she had no idea who I was."

Chapter 8

Aura stood on the small stone patio in her backyard, the three amulets she had collected lined up on the glass-topped table before her. In the thick hedges surrounding the patio, crickets chirped and night birds sang their romantic melodies. A cool breeze ruffled the hem of her long white skirt, tickling her skin. Aura smiled serenely. One more amulet and her destiny was complete. One more, and then there would be no more parlor tricks or small-time witchcraft for her. Four amulets, four witches. Soon she would have everything she needed to wield her awesome power over the Earth.

The back door opened and Delilah stepped out, followed by Terra, who closed the door behind them with a soft click. A full moon lit the patio, bathing their faces in a cool, mystical glow. Aura took a deep breath of the clean air as her friends joined her.

"How is she?" Aura asked, lifting the first

amulet from the table and fingering its cool surface.

"She's fine," Terra said. She sat down at the
table and gave a sigh, her shoulders rounding.

"She's taking a bath, the little prima donna,"
Delilah added.

"Good," Aura said. "Let her regroup, get her
strength back. Then we can go after the fourth
amulet."

"Finally," Delilah said.

"Yes," Aura agreed with a smile. "Before you
know it, our mission will be complete. We are
finally going to do what all those witches from
years ago were too afraid to do. We're going to
be all-powerful."

Terra sighed again, more obviously, and sat
back hard in her chair. Aura and Delilah
exchanged an impatient look. Somehow, Aura
got the feeling that Terra was having second
thoughts.

"What's with the negative vibes, Terra?"
Aura asked her, walking around to the other
side of the table so she could face her friend.
"Isn't everything going according to plan? Just
like I said it would?"

"I don't know, you guys," Terra said. "I have
a bad feeling."

Delilah snorted and yanked out a chair, plop-
ping down into it. "You always have a bad feeling."

"It's just, did you see Paige's powers?" Terra

said, her dark eyes wide. "She almost killed you, Aura. She *could* have killed you!"

"No, she couldn't," Aura said, rolling her eyes.

"Please! If she'd hit you with that thing a little harder, you'd be in a coma right now," Terra told her.

Aura scoffed. Yes, she had a lump the size of a grapefruit on the back of her head, and all her muscles still hurt from being so unexpectedly jarred, but Terra and Delilah didn't need to know that. All that mattered was that she was fine. And she would be even better once she gave it back to that little witch tenfold.

"So why didn't she?" Aura said, lifting her shoulders. "Why didn't she take me out?"

Terra stared at her blankly.

"I'll tell you why," Aura said. "Because she didn't have the guts. I'm already more powerful than that hack because I have the courage to follow through. *She* was probably too worried that I might be an Innocent. That I might somehow be turned or saved. She doesn't have it in her to finish the job."

"I don't know. I think she might have just been holding back because she was afraid Phoebe could get caught in the crossfire," Terra theorized. "And if she has that kind of power when she's alone, imagine what it'll be like when she has her sister with her." Terra pulled at one of her curls and toyed with it, shaking her head. "There's no way we can take them, you guys. I don't know what we were thinking. I mean, they're the *Charmed Ones*."

"Yeah, and they're down one sister," Delilah pointed out. "*We* have her now."

"The Power of Three no longer exists," Aura added, savoring the taste of those words on her tongue.

"But for how long?" Terra said, pushing away from the table. She got up and started pacing the perimeter of the patio. "What if her memory comes back? You heard what Paige said to her. What if something she said sparks a memory?"

"That is true," Delilah said, raising her eyebrows. "All that crap Paige was spewing about being her sister. It might get her thinking."

"Not you, too," Aura said, frustrated.

"Well, what if it does?" Terra whined. "What if she turns on us? What then?"

"That's why we have to get the fourth amulet quickly, before she does remember," Aura told her. "Once we have it, we'll be able to vanquish Paige and Piper, and then Phoebe—or should I say 'Ruth'—will be one of us forever. She'll have no choice."

"She's going to figure it out," Terra said tremulously. "There's no way we can win."

"All right, I've had about enough of this negativity," Aura said to Terra, squaring off with her. "What are you going to do, Terra? Run scared?"

"So, what if I am?" Terra asked, her eyes

flashing. "I *am* scared. And you should be too. I don't understand how you can stand there and not be worried. These are our lives we're talking about here."

Aura stared Terra down. She should have known that this would happen. Terra had always had a weak constitution, but Aura had kept her around because Terra knew everything there was to know about witchcraft and potions and the mystical realm. She had thought that if Terra could see the kind of power Aura was offering her, that eventually she would toughen up and get behind the cause. But, apparently, Aura had been wrong.

And Aura hated being wrong.

Unfortunately, there was nothing she could do about it now. It wasn't like she could just look up "Witches" in the yellow pages and find a new one to complete their chain. It was either Terra, or failure. And failure was not an option.

"You're not leaving," Aura told her firmly. "This is what I was meant to do. What we were *all* meant to do. You're not walking out on us now just because you got a little spooked. Not when we're so close."

"Maybe I am," Terra said, lifting her chin. "What are you going to do about it?"

Aura glanced over her shoulder at Delilah, who instantly rose to stand by her side. Together, they faced Terra.

"Oh, I don't know. Kill you?" Aura said.

Terra took a step back, her face ashen. But she forced herself to laugh. "Yeah, right. You wouldn't hurt me," she said.

"No?"

Aura thrust out her hand and focused everything she had on her power. She had no idea if this was actually going to work, but she had to believe it would. Each time she joined hands with her sister witches and said the connection spell, she felt a bit stronger, a bit more indestructible. She had a feeling that thanks to the amulets, her power had started growing on its own, and now it was time to test it.

Aura lifted her hand, and Terra levitated off the ground.

"What are you doing?" Terra asked, only mildly alarmed. "You can't do this!"

She was only a few inches above the ground, her toes nearly grazing the patio floor, but as Aura held her breath and poured all of her energy into her power, Terra started to rise. She let out a yelp of surprise as she rose higher and higher into the air, until she was suspended at least six feet above Aura's head.

"Aura! What are you doing? Let me down!" Terra cried.

Delilah whistled, impressed. "Wow, girl. How are you doing that?"

Aura's whole body was trembling from the strain, and she fought to keep it under control. "Still think I won't do it?" she asked Terra through her teeth.

"I'm sorry, all right?" Terra shouted. "I'll do whatever you want. Just, please, don't drop me."

"You swear?" Aura asked.

"Yes! I swear! I swear!" Terra cried, starting to panic.

"You'd better let her down before Phoebe hears her," Delilah whispered.

Aura sighed. She had to let go anyway, or she was going to drain herself completely. Slowly, deliberately, she lowered Terra to the ground. As soon as Terra's feet hit the slate floor, the girl collapsed in a heap, crying in relief. Aura staggered back and fell into a chair, gasping for breath. Never in her life had she felt so weak and so triumphant all at once.

"Are you both okay?" Delilah asked, looking from Aura to Terra and back.

"Yes," Terra said tearfully.

"I will be," Aura said, sucking wind.

Delilah extended her hand to Terra, who clasped it gratefully. She pulled Terra to her feet, and took a deep breath.

"You're with us now, right?" she said, staring Terra in the eye. "No matter what?"

Terra looked past her at Aura, who mustered what little energy she had left to give her a no-nonsense glare.

Just try me, Aura thought, clenching her hands into fists.

"Yes," Terra said grimly. "No matter what."

"Good." Delilah clapped her hands together.

"Now let's go pay another visit to our premonition machine. It's about time we found that last amulet. Before we all self-destruct."

"One more time, lass, and you've got 'em!" Teague shouted, crouching behind the overturned dining room table with Piper.

There was a shout, and the satyr went flying over their heads, landing in a heap near the kitchen door. His flute flew out of his hands and shattered into a dozen pieces on the floor. The nymphs raced to his side to tend to him, while the giant clubbed the offending Flecter over the head.

"How are you keeping track of this?" Piper asked Teague.

"I'm a leprechaun. We have a good head for numbers," he said, tapping his temple. "One more time's the charm. Trust me."

"If you say so." Piper jumped up and blasted the Flecter with her power once more. He wavered and staggered back, then shouted in anger and burst into flame. His passing left a dark scorch mark on the flowered wallpaper.

"Nice one!" the dwarf called out, ducking into a somersault to avoid another Flecter's energy ball.

Paige shot the ball back at the demon, taking him out as well, but two more Flecters immediately appeared to take their place. And somehow, they looked even angrier than the demons that had come before them.

"What're we going to do?" Paige cried, taking cover with Piper. "They won't stop coming!"

"I don't understand! We've killed dozens of them already," Piper groused, wincing as another fireball exploded against the wall. "Why have we not gotten the emperor yet? Didn't Phoebe say that was the key?"

"A' course that's the key! Everyone knows you have to kill a Flecter's emperor," Brian shouted from across the room, where he and Gail were deflecting energy balls with their staffs. "But what do you think? They're gonna bring their weakness right *to* you?"

"He's right. *You* have to go to *him*," Teague said. "You're gonna have to find the leader on your own."

"Well, how do we do that?" Piper asked over the din of the battle.

"With a simple locator spell, I'm sure," Teague replied. "But once you find him, you'll need the Power of Three to vanquish him. There's no doubt about that."

"Great," Piper said through her teeth. "Why am I not surprised?"

"Here comes another! You've gotten this one two times already! Just hit him once more!" Teague shouted.

Piper groaned and shoved herself up again. She found herself facing three Flecters, all of whom were snarling at her.

"Which one?" she cried.

"Hit all of 'em!" Teague shouted back.

Piper hit the first and the second. As the second one exploded, the third pulled back and launched his energy ball at her, but Paige grabbed her at the last second and orbed her out. They reappeared in the kitchen, and Piper let out a breath of relief.

"This is insane. We can't do this without Phoebe," she said.

The two nymphs finally stood up in the doorway, dragging the now blinking satyr with them. He rubbed his head and tried to focus, but nearly fell over.

"Is he okay?" Paige asked.

"We think so," one of the nymphs replied, running her fingers lovingly over the satyr's hand.

Piper blinked and looked around. "It's awfully quiet in there all of a sudden," she said.

Paige and Piper turned and walked back into the living room. The walls and floor were scorched and smoldering. The curtains had been incinerated, and all the furniture had been knocked over or blown to smithereens. From behind the couch and chairs and out of every corner crept their magical friends, glancing around to make sure that the danger really had passed. Teague stepped out from behind a potted plant, his brow glistening with sweat.

"What happened?" Piper asked.

"Think we scared 'em off for now," Teague said, wiping his forehead with a handkerchief.

"But they said they'd be back," the giant told them. His tatty robes were covered with burn marks. Otherwise, he looked none the worse for the wear.

"Of course they did," Paige said.

"Okay. That's it," Piper said, stepping over the furniture carnage on her way to the front door.

"Where are you going?" Paige asked, following after her.

"*We* are going to go find Phoebe and bring her back here," Piper said. "You heard Teague. We can't vanquish these Flecters without her, and we certainly can't keep fighting them off like this. Pretty soon, we're not even going to have a house anymore."

"But how are we going to find her?" Paige asked. "We've already tried everything."

"Yes, but now you know who she's with," Piper told Paige, grabbing both their jackets off the floor, where they had fallen during the fight. "Which means we can do things the old-fashioned way."

Paige took her jacket and yanked it on as Piper held open the door. "What if the Flecters come back while we're gone?" she asked.

"Don't worry about it a bit!" Teague told them with a wink. "We'll hold down the fort. You just worry about finding your sister."

Piper smiled. "Thank you, Teague."

Teague nodded humbly. "'Tis the least we can do after causing you all so much trouble."

"Don't worry about it. We're glad you were here to help," Piper replied. "And with any luck, we'll be back with the sister you were supposed to see in the first place."

"Luck? Luck I can help you with," Teague said with a twinkle in his eye.

He opened his hand to reveal a nugget of leprechaun gold. "*Sláinte is táinte,*" he said quietly.

Suddenly, Piper felt a rush of warmth and confidence. Paige grinned. Nothing like a little luck of the Irish to get a girl going again.

"Come on," Piper said, tossing her hair over her shoulders. "Let's go find Phoebe."

Paige sat in a cracked vinyl chair in the corner of the bustling police station, trying as best she could to recall any details of Phoebe's new "friends." Across the metal desk, Officer Bright, a young woman with dark skin and hundreds of tiny braids, sketched away on a large pad, bringing Paige's descriptions to life. She had already finished her drawings of two of the girls, the dark-haired one and the one with braids, and they had both come out perfectly. Now Paige was working on a description of the last member of the menacing trio, the one who had the sick power of levitation. Not that Officer Bright needed to know that particular detail.

"Her hair was long and straight," Paige said, squinting as she tried to picture the girl. "It was parted on the right side," she added.

This she knew for sure, since she had been looking *down* at the girl's part from eight feet above her head. Paige took a sip of water from the plastic cup the officer had given her, and glanced across the room at Piper, who was seated on the couch near the wall with Darryl Morris, their one friend inside the San Francisco Police Department. Piper winced as Darryl taped gauze over the wound on her arm. A far cry from being healed by her Whitelighter husband, but Piper had refused to call Leo. She wanted him to stay with Wyatt, wherever they were, so that they both would be out of harm's way.

"Okay, what about her eyes?" Officer Bright asked, glancing up from her work.

The room was full of ringing phones, and cops shouting and laughing with one another. Paige had no idea how the poor woman could concentrate in this noisy atmosphere.

"They were dark, and had kind of an almond shape," Paige told her, raising her voice to be heard over some guy in handcuffs who was ranting about his innocence. "Sort of mysterious. But also determined. Strong."

"Good. Good," Officer Bright said. "That's exactly the kind of thing I need. You wouldn't believe how many people come in here and say,

'Their eyes were brown.' Makes my job a lot harder."

"Well, I do what I can," Paige said with a smile.

"Okay," Officer Bright replied, putting the finishing touches on her drawing. She turned the sketch pad around and showed it to Paige. "Is this her?"

"Yes! That looks exactly like her," Paige said. "You're good."

"Thanks," Officer Bright said with a grin.

Darryl walked over and took the sketch pad from Officer Bright. He laid it out next to the other drawings on the desk. As he looked down at them, he blew out a sigh.

"They don't exactly look like a dangerous gang, do they?" he asked, smoothing his tie.

"Believe me, they are," Paige said with a shudder. Her time suspended in the air had not been easy.

"Looks can be deceiving," Piper told him. "I think we figured that one out a long time ago."

"Good point," Darryl said. He patted Officer Bright on the back as she stood. "Nice work. Thank you. We'll send these out to all the other station houses and maybe to the colleges in town as well. They look like they might be students at one of the universities."

"That's it?" Piper asked, gingerly moving her arm around, testing its strength.

"Well, we can also run the sketches through the computer system, but without fingerprints it'll take a lot longer to find a match. We're talking days," Darryl told them. "Are you sure you have nothing else to go on, Paige?"

"No. I'm sorry," Paige said. "But run that one first," she told him, pointing at the newest sketch. "I think she was the leader."

"You got it," Darryl said.

A young cop, blond and innocent-looking in his blue rookie uniform, paused as he walked by, his eye caught by the sketch. "Excuse me, Inspector," he said to Darryl. "Mind if I take a look at that?"

Paige and Piper exchanged a look. Paige felt her pulse start to quicken. She stood up from her chair. Was it possible that this cop knew who their witch was?

"Why? Do you recognize this woman, Officer Palmer?" Darryl asked.

The cop held the sketch pad in both hands and studied it. "Yeah. Yeah, I do. We questioned her a couple of weeks ago," Officer Palmer said with a nod. "An elderly lady accused her of stealing this necklace from her bedroom. I think the woman was actually her grandmother, if I recall correctly. Yeah. The girl had gone for a visit at the lady's retirement home and the necklace went missing. The grandmother was convinced the girl took it, but there was no way of knowing for sure. It was 'she said, she said,' you know? We just figured it was a family dispute and they would settle it on their own."

"Stealing a necklace?" Paige asked. She suddenly recalled another detail of her bizarre encounter with Phoebe and her band of witches. One of the girls had been holding a necklace, possibly some kind of charm.

"Yeah. It was a family heirloom or something," Officer Palmer told them. "The woman was pretty freaked about it. I guess the amulet meant a lot to her."

"An amulet? She used that word?" Piper asked.

"Yeah. That was what she kept calling it," he said with a shrug.

Paige felt goosebumps pop up all along her arms. The plot was beginning to thicken. If the necklace really was an amulet, then it might hold some kind of power.

"Got any paperwork on the suspect?" Daryl asked.

"Sure. I save everything, just in case," the young cop said, walking over to his desk. "You never know, right?"

Thank you, Teague, Paige thought as she and Piper hovered over the officer's desk. This happy little coincidence had "leprechaun luck" written all over it.

Officer Palmer pulled a couple of folders out of his bottom desk drawer and rifled through them. After what seemed like an eternity of flipping and sifting, he finally yanked out a white form.

"Here we go. Her name is Aura Chen. There's her address," he said, holding out the sheet of paper.

Darryl reached out for the form, but Piper snatched it from the young officer's grasp before he ever got near it.

"I know exactly where this is," she said, glancing at the address. "Let's go."

Paige grabbed her purse and took off after Piper.

"Wait! Where are you going?" Darryl called after them.

Paige turned around on her way out the door. "We're gonna go save our sister."

Chapter 9

Ruth sighed and lifted the stopper in the bathtub. Instantly the water around her started to drain, taking the plump, rose-scented bubbles with it. She wished she could have stayed in the comforting warmth of the bath forever, but, after a while, it had started to grow cooler and soon she knew it would freeze her out. Better to get out now, before it left her cold.

She used a thick white towel to dry off, then wrapped herself up in her plush robe with the elaborate *R* embroidered on the pocket. All she needed now was a good night's sleep. It had been an insane day. So insane that it had left her wondering if her life was actually always like this. Before her amnesia, had she really run around fighting bad witches and working for the greater good? It seemed like something a person would remember.

But, even if it *was* a crazy existence, at least she had a purpose. At least she was helping the world become a better place.

Stepping in front of the mirror, Ruth used the sleeve of her robe to wipe away some of the condensation. She stared at her reflection, thinking about her encounter with the evil witch in the alley that afternoon—the fact that the girl had called Ruth her sister. Every time Ruth thought about it, she got chills. But it couldn't be true, right? If she had a sister who was an evil witch, Aura would have told her about it. Ruth had to trust Aura. She had to believe that her truest friend wouldn't lie to her that way.

It was just a mind game, like Aura said, Ruth thought. *That girl was just trying to mess with me.*

Ruth examined her face in the mirror, turning left, then right. Her heart thumped painfully in her chest as she realized that there was a certain resemblance between herself and the evil witch. But they *couldn't* be sisters. There was just no way. The girl was a bad witch, and as far as Ruth could tell, *she* didn't have an evil bone in her body.

But where *had* she gotten her brown hair, her gold-flecked eyes? Ruth had spent hours staring at the one picture she had of her with her parents. She didn't see much family resemblance between her and them. Had her straight teeth come from someone in her family, or had she worn braces? What was the significance of the tattoo on her shoulder? Would she ever know?

Tomorrow, she promised herself. Tomorrow she would get Aura and the others to tell her

more about her past. If she had really known
Aura for so long, then Aura had to have the
answers to some of these questions. She would
have to be able to tell her something more about
where Ruth had come from.

The only thing she knew for sure was that she
couldn't be related to the evil witch. Because
that would mean that she, Ruth, might have
been evil at some point. And she wanted to be
good. She wanted to fight with her friends on
the right side. Evil held no interest for her.

There was a quick rap on the door before
Aura, Delilah, and Terra entered the large bathroom. The moment they walked in, the bathtub
finished emptying, letting out a long, sucking
squeal as it drained the last of the bubbles away.

"Hi," Ruth said uncertainly, holding the robe
closer to herself. She retied the belt more
securely around her waist. "What's the matter?"

"Sorry to interrupt, but we need to see if you
can get another premonition," Aura said, stepping forward while the others hovered near the
door.

She held out the amulet they had taken that
afternoon. Ruth stared down at it. Her body was
so tired and her head felt as if all it could handle
just then was a comfy pillow. Hadn't she put
herself through enough for one day?

"Now?" she asked, biting her lip. She
dreaded the feeling that overcame her with each
premonition, that seizing of her muscles—the

complete surrender of control. "I thought we were going to wait on that."

"Well, we can't," Delilah said flatly. "We need the power."

"The power?" Ruth asked.

Aura glanced over her shoulder at Delilah. "She means, we need to take the power from the last of the evil witches," Aura explained. "She must know by now that we've collected the other amulets. If she does, then she might panic and try to use it as much as possible before we come for her."

"Who knows what she might do with it?" Terra threw in.

Aura nodded grimly. "Please, Ruth. We need to stop her before she hurts someone. This is the last time, we promise. As soon as we have this amulet safely in our possession, it will all be over."

Ruth looked around at her friends. They were watching her with such optimism, such belief. As if she were their only hope. How could she possibly let them down? Especially after all they had done for her. All they had given her and taught her.

"Okay," she said finally.

Aura squeezed Ruth's shoulder in thanks and handed over the amulet. Ruth walked over to the chair in front of the vanity table and sat down. She placed the amulet between both her palms and closed her eyes. For a long moment, nothing happened. At first Ruth was relieved. Maybe this amulet would bring no visions. Maybe she had been granted a reprieve.

"Concentrate," Aura urged quietly. "Connect with the power."

Ruth took a deep breath and let it out through her nose. She reached out with her mind and tried to think about nothing but the amulet. Almost immediately, she felt the premonition coming on. Her breath caught, and in a swirl of dizzying color, she was entranced.

The scene played out before her much like the others had. Ruth was standing in the center of a large, airy apartment. Books and magazines were strewn everywhere and lamps and clocks were overturned, as if an earthquake had just hit. A powerful-looking woman of about sixty, wearing a flowing dress, fell to her knees in front of Delilah. Then Terra appeared as if from nowhere and handed the fourth amulet over to Aura. Aura grasped the token and lifted it with a triumphant smile. Then the vision ended, and Ruth was returned to the real world with a jolt.

She opened her eyes slowly. Everything came back into focus in a rush.

"Well? What did you see?" Aura asked, kneeling in front of her.

"I saw an older woman," Ruth said shakily. "She was very powerful, but we fought her and won."

"I like it already," Delilah said, rubbing her

hands together. "So, where is she? Where do we go?"

"I . . . I don't know," Ruth told them, trying to concentrate. "We were in her apartment this time. There was no address. No sign. She could be anywhere."

"You're kidding," Delilah said.

"Oh, well," Terra put in, turning to go. "Guess that's it, then."

"No, that is not it," Aura said, glaring at her. She focused her intense gaze on Ruth and clutched her hand. "Think back. Was there anything in the apartment? Anything at all that can help us?"

"Yeah, like a utility bill?" Delilah joked.

A rush of hope shot through Ruth's chest. "Wait a minute. There were magazines."

"Good! Magazines!" Aura said hungrily. "Were any of them subscriptions? Can you see an address?"

Ruth sat back and closed her eyes, bringing her hands to her head. She tried to focus on the magazines on the floor. Tried to see the labels curling from the covers.

Come on, Ruth, you can do it, she told herself. *Don't let them down.*

Then it came to her, seemingly out of the ether. A name. The name at the top of an address label. It scrolled in front of her like a headline on the evening news.

"Maribel Locke," she whispered aloud. When

she opened her eyes, Aura was gazing up at her. "Her name is Maribel Locke."

Slowly, Aura's mouth twisted into a satisfied, determined grin. She squeezed Ruth's hand once, then stood. "Terra, go check the phone book. See if you can find our Ms. Locke," she said, her eyes gleaming.

Terra turned—quite slowly, Ruth noticed— and left the room. Ruth could hear her reluctant footsteps on the wooden stairs outside, and wondered what was wrong. Didn't Terra want to find this woman as much as Aura and Delilah did?

"Good work, Ruth," Aura said gently. "Now you'd better get dressed. We have one more witch to take down."

"Okay, I've worked out the locator spell for the Flecters' emperor," Paige said as Piper drove her Jeep Cherokee through the streets of San Francisco, seriously breaking the speed limit. "Once we get Phoebe back, this should work."

"Nice. And Leo should be working on the vanquishing potion right now," Piper said. "Now all we need is the Power of Three."

"The power of two is just never enough, is it?" Paige joked, clearly trying to lighten the mood.

Piper didn't even try to smile. "Put the spell somewhere safe while we do this."

Paige folded up the paper she had jotted her

spell on and shoved it into her pocket just as
Piper pulled the SUV to a stop. The sisters
looked up at the stucco façade of Aura Chen's
house. The palm trees out front swayed in the
breeze and the tiny lights along the walk seemed
to wink. It looked like a day spa, not the home of
an evil coven.

"This is it?" Paige said. "What is it, a million-
aire cult?"

"A lot of cults are, from what I've heard,"
Piper said, removing her seatbelt.

"Wait. What're you doing?" Paige said, grabbing Piper's forearm.

"I'm going in," Piper told her. "Strike that.
We're going in."

"Don't you want to stake it out first or something?" Paige suggested. "Get the lay of the
land? You know, see what we're dealing with."

Piper leveled her with a sarcastic stare.
"Paige, they've got Phoebe in there. You can sit
in the car and play detective, but I am going into
that house, and dragging her out if I have to."

"And she says *I'm* rash," Paige said under her
breath.

Piper ignored her and got out of the car, slamming the door behind her. She knew what she
was doing. So Paige had seen these girls use
some wicked powers. Piper had been up against
worse. Her power trumped any other witch's
power, any day of the week. Of that she was
sure.

Piper started up the front walk, checking the windows for spies. Every one of them was shuttered. A car door closed behind her and she heard Paige scurrying to catch up.

"What're you going to do? Ring the bell and ask if Phoebe can come out and play?" Paige said as they approached the door.

Piper paused. "Actually, that's not the worst plan."

She lifted her fist to rap on the door, but her knuckles never touched the paneled surface. About a centimeter before they would have met the wood, her arm was thrust backward with a jerk. Suddenly, Piper was hit by a blast of power to her chest and thrown off her feet. She shouted in surprise as she was tossed through the air and blown right past Paige, who tried in vain to grab her. With a slam, Piper landed flat on her side on the slate walkway.

Okay. That hurt, Piper thought, attempting to breathe, but coughing instead.

"Piper! Are you okay!?" Paige asked, crouching at her side.

Tentatively, Piper lifted her head. A stab of pain shot through her skull and she groaned.

"No, I'm not okay," she said, frustrated.

With Paige's help, she turned over onto her back and propped herself up on her hands. She could feel a scrape on her forehead and a warm trickle of blood making its way along her temple.

"Ouch. That looks bad," Paige said.

"What the hell *was* that?" Piper asked, scrambling to her feet. Her mind went fuzzy for a second and she grasped Paige to steady herself, waiting for the dizziness to pass.

"I'd say they've put a protection spell on their house," Paige offered, looking up at the shuttered windows. "A pretty kickass one."

"Those little witches," Piper said, incredulous.

"Told you they were packing some power," Paige said.

"Well, let's see if they can protect against *this*," Piper said, storming forward.

"Piper! No!" Paige shouted.

Piper thrust out her hands and shot her power at the door. There was a loud *bang*, but nothing exploded. Instead, the house's power erupted once again and tossed Piper back even farther than before. This time, she smacked the back of her head against the cold, hard slate. It was as if her own power had been deflected back at her. And it *hurt*.

"Are you trying to get yourself killed?" Paige cried, hovering over her.

"Apparently," Piper said.

She shook her head and sat up slowly. The whole world was swimming before her, moving up and down in undulating waves. Paige's face dissolved and reformed before her eyes, over and over and over again.

"Okay. This is not good," Piper said.

"Tell me about it," Paige said. "Can you stand?"

"I think so," Piper said.

She reached for her sister's hands, and together they got her to her feet. Piper stared at the front door and felt as if it were mocking her. She couldn't remember the last time she had had trouble getting into a plain old house. Demon lairs, maybe. Dungeons, sure. But not a regular suburban house.

"What're we gonna do now?" Paige asked.

"I don't know," Piper answered. "But I am not leaving here until we get Phoebe away from these psychos."

Just then, the front door swung open, and out traipsed three girls—the very three Paige had described for the sketch artist at the station house. They turned right and headed for the driveway, apparently not even realizing they had visitors. Had they not noticed one of the most powerful witches on Earth trying to blast their front door down?

"Hey!" Piper shouted, stepping forward.

All three of them stopped, at the very moment Phoebe walked through the front doorway. Aura and her dark-haired friend smirked at Piper like she was some kind of joke. It got right under her skin.

"We've got company," the dark-haired girl sang.

Phoebe took one look at Piper and blanched.

Piper half expected her sister to run to her side, but, instead, she rushed over to the other girls, as if hoping for their protection.

"Phoebe!" Piper said, a sliver cutting right through her heart. "It's me!"

"Told you she didn't remember us," Paige said through her teeth.

"Screw that. She's known me her entire life. I'm her big sister," Piper said, stepping forward. "Phoebe!" she said. "Wake up, already. It's me, Piper. We've come to take you home."

"Ignore her," the dark-haired girl said to Phoebe. "She's evil. She's just trying to win you to their side."

"I know," Phoebe said firmly. "But I know where I belong."

"Yes, so do I! With us!" Piper called out. "The Power of Three, remember? Your destiny?"

The way that Phoebe just stared at Piper blankly chilled Piper's heart. How could her sister not remember all the good they had done, all the battles they had won together? How could Phoebe not remember *her*? They had only spent their entire lives together, laughing and bickering and borrowing clothes and talking about everything. Phoebe had been the one to find the Book of Shadows in the first place, to recite the incantation that had brought the sisters' powers to them. It had been one of the most important moments of their lives, and, clearly, Phoebe had no recollection of it whatsoever. Piper had no idea that Phoebe's amnesia would hurt this much. Suddenly she felt so overcome, it was as if she weighed a thousand pounds.

Aura grinned. "Let's do it," she said.

"Do what?" Piper snapped, mostly to keep the tears at bay.

Phoebe reached out and took the hand of the girl nearest to her.

"We four stand, hand in hand, forming an impenetrable band," the girls recited. A hot wind kicked up, swirling dust and dirt into Piper's eyes.

"Phoebe! What're you doing? This is ridiculous!" Piper sputtered, spitting her hair off her lips.

"Let their powers fuel my own. Let us all have powers grown."

"Piper! Watch out!" Paige shouted.

Piper shoved her hair out of her face and looked at Aura just as she dropped her friends' hands. The girl raised her fingers into the air, and suddenly Piper flew up into the sky, her legs dangling, her heart jumping into her throat.

"Whoa! What is this?" Piper shouted, her arms flailing. So much for weighing a thousand pounds. It seemed she was light as air. The pathway lights glimmered below her as she kicked her feet, desperately trying to find ground. Aura grinned up at her giddily.

"Piper!" Paige called out, lifting her hand,

trying to orb her down. Nothing happened. Paige glanced at Aura, surprised.

Why didn't that work? Piper wondered, her stomach swooping. *Is this girl's power stronger than Paige's?*

"Piper!" Paige tried again. Nothing.

"Well, isn't *that* interesting?" Aura said with a smirk.

All at once, Piper no longer felt depressed. She was right back in fighting mode.

"Let me down, you *witch*!" Piper shouted.

"Soon enough," Aura called back. "Right now, we have someplace to be. Come on, girls."

She turned and headed for the SUV parked in the driveway.

"Later," the dark-haired girl called up to Piper.

Phoebe cast her one last look before following after her new friends. A look with zero recognition in it. A look that told Piper she'd be back, and she'd be out for blood.

There was the sound of an engine revving, and then the SUV sped out of the driveway, peeling out in the street. Piper hung there, ego bruised, feeling totally defeated. Feeling as though her little sister had just stabbed her in the back.

"You okay?" Paige called up to her.

"Fine," Piper replied. "Think you could try again?"

Paige reached up one hand. "Piper," she said.

The next thing Piper knew, she was landing softly on the ground. "Thanks," she said, dusting herself off. "Why didn't it work the first two times?"

"I guess her power's growing," Paige said. "I think it was deflecting mine."

"Well, that can't be good," Piper said.

"No, it can't. What now?" Paige asked.

Piper took a deep breath and looked down the street after the witches' car. Never in her life had she wanted to strangle another witch quite so badly. "Now we go home and come up with plan B."

"You guys, tell me the truth," Ruth said, sitting forward in the backseat and clutching Delilah's headrest. "I'm not really related to those people, am I? I'm not evil."

Terra stared out the side window as the lights in the windows blurred by. Up front, Aura and Delilah exchanged a look. Ruth's heart gave a thump of foreboding.

"No, sweetie, you're not related to those girls. And you're not evil," Aura said, catching Ruth's eye in the rearview mirror. "If you were evil, you wouldn't be able to fight against those witches. They would suck you right in. Turn you against us. But they haven't been able to do that so far."

"You're sure?" Ruth said, feeling slightly better.

"Absolutely," Aura said. "I told you, I've known

you since we were kids. I think I'd remember if you had two evil sisters."

"True," Ruth said. She took a deep breath and sat back. "So I'm definitely a good witch. No doubt about it."

"Of course you are," Delilah told her, looking at her in the mirror. "You know I can read thoughts and auras, right?"

Ruth nodded.

"Well, I haven't read a single dark vibe off you since we met," Delilah told her, turning in her seat.

"Really?" Ruth said hopefully, raising her eyebrows.

"I promise," Delilah told her. "Believe me. You are *not* bad."

Delilah settled back into her seat and she and Aura grinned. Ruth was finally able to relax. As long as her friends believed in her, she had no reason not to believe in herself.

"Did you see how shocked she was when she saw my power?" Aura asked, bringing the SUV to a stop at a red light. "I thought she was going to faint."

"It *was* pretty cool," Delilah agreed.

"I cannot wait until I can do that on my own—You know, without becoming a total vegetable afterward," Aura said, slamming on the gas again as the light turned green. "No offense, but reciting that little incantation every time is getting old."

"Aside from the fact that it takes up way too much time," Delilah added.

"What do you mean, you can't wait until you can do it on your own?" Phoebe asked.

For a moment, there was nothing but silence inside the car, no sounds except the whoosh of the cars rushing by outside. Finally, Terra sighed.

"You'll see," she said, lifting her head away from the window momentarily. "Soon enough, you'll see."

Chapter 10

"Okay, here we go," Aura said, as the four girls gathered on the front step of Maribel Locke's apartment building. The old, converted Victorian stood on a quiet San Francisco street, where it seemed most of the families were already in for the night, eating dinner behind their plate-glass windows. "Is everyone ready?"

Ruth nodded resolutely along with Terra and Delilah. Her blood raced through her veins so fast she thought her heart might give out at any second. She couldn't wait for this to be over. Aura had said this was the last battle. Ruth hoped that her friend was sure about that.

"How are we going in? Want me to pick the lock?" Delilah asked, stepping forward. She drew from her pants pocket a thin, black leather case, full of tiny tools.

"You know how to pick locks?" Ruth asked.

"Little skill I picked up in juvie," Delilah said

with a shrug. "There's a lot you don't know about me."

Apparently, Ruth thought. Somehow, breaking and entering didn't seem right. Even if it *was* an evil witch's apartment.

"Actually, I thought Ruth might get us in," Aura said, turning her hopeful eyes on Ruth. "The door looks pretty flimsy. Think you could kick it down?" she asked.

"I . . . I don't know," Ruth said. "Wouldn't Delilah's way be more subtle?"

"Yes, but it would take longer, and Maribel might hear us," Aura said. "This way, we have the element of surprise on our side. If she's as powerful as you said she is, we're going to need every advantage we can get."

"You can do it, Ruth," Delilah said, pocketing her tools.

"Really?" Ruth was skeptical.

"We've seen you do it before," Terra offered. "You kick some serious butt."

Ruth had gotten a sense of her fighting powers earlier that day in the alley, but she hadn't truly tested them out yet. Part of her felt like this was wrong, but how could it be? They were here to take down a force of evil. And her friends were all counting on her.

"I guess I'll give it a try," she said. "Everyone step back."

They did as they were told and Ruth stared at the doorknob, just hoping she'd get this right.

One misfire and she could really hurt herself. With one swift motion, she lifted her foot and slammed it into the space just below the doorknob. The entire door jam splintered and the door shot open, slamming back against the wall.

I did it! I can't believe I did it! Ruth thought.

"Nice work!" Delilah cheered.

"Let's go," Aura said, striding inside.

Terra gave Ruth an encouraging smile as she walked into the building. Ruth took a deep breath and followed. But, before she got to the inside door, she heard a shout of surprise. Suddenly, Aura came flying out of the apartment and tumbled to the hallway floor, followed by a rain of heavy hardcover books. Ruth crouched on the floor, shielding her face with her arms.

"Are you okay?" she asked Aura.

"You didn't tell us she was telekinetic!" Aura said through her teeth. "Duck!"

Ruth flattened herself to the ground just as a ceramic lamp flew past her head. It shattered against the wall behind her, shooting shards of white glass everywhere.

"I didn't know!" Ruth cried, helping Aura to her feet. "In my vision, all I saw was our defeating her."

"Well, then, let's do that," Aura said, determined.

They clutched hands and together rushed into the fray. Delilah was pinned to the wall in the living room, two decorative swords piercing her blouse and holding her hands against her sides. Terra was huddled behind the couch, trembling, as knickknacks and books flew all around her. Ruth took one look at the old witch standing in the middle of the room and knew that she was willing the couch to move and crush Terra. There was no way Ruth was going to let that happen. She raced into the room, launched herself into the air, and took the witch down with one swift kick. The woman reeled and hit the floor, a mass of gray hair and flowered dress. All the flying books and statues and lamps and frames fell to the ground with a cacophonous crash. Meanwhile, Aura ran to the other side of the room and freed Delilah.

Ruth stood over the witch, making sure she wouldn't get up again. The woman turned over onto her side and looked up at Ruth shakily. Her blue eyes widened in recognition.

"You!" she cried. "I know you!"

In that moment, Ruth forgot why she was there. She forgot that she was supposed to be taking this woman down. All she felt was a rush of hope.

"You do?" she asked.

"Yes!" the woman said, pushing herself up off the floor. "You were here a few months ago with your sisters. You saved me from that soul-sucking demon. Why are you attacking me?" she asked, clearly confused. "How could you do this?"

Ruth's mouth dropped open, but nothing came out. This woman looked so desperate. So confused. And she was talking gibberish. There was no way she could know Ruth, was there?

She turned around to ask Aura if she knew anything about this. Aura had already locked hands with Delilah and Terra, and they were walking across all the debris toward Ruth.

"We're doing this because you are evil," Aura said to the woman, grabbing Ruth's hand.

"What are you talking about?" the woman asked, backing away. "This has to be some kind of mistake. You can't do this."

"Watch us," Delilah said.

"Ready?" Aura said, squeezing Ruth's fingers.

"She . . . she says she knows me," Ruth said uncertainly. "What if she's not evil?"

"Evil!" the witch exclaimed. "*Evil*?"

"Don't you trust me, Ruth?" Aura asked. "Have I ever led you astray?"

"No," Ruth said, though she didn't put much conviction behind it. This was all too confusing.

"Then recite the spell," Aura demanded.

Ruth turned and looked at the witch on the floor. She had seen this happening in her vision. She knew that it was supposed to be. There was no way she could fight it. It had to be the right thing. It just had to be.

Finally, she nodded, and the girls began to chant.

"We four stand, hand in hand, forming an impenetrable band," Ruth recited with her friends.

Like a cannon shot, all the books still on the shelves came flying at them from every direction. One heavy tome slammed into Ruth's foot. Another hit her left hand and almost wrenched her fingers from Aura's grasp.

"Don't break the bond!" Aura shouted over all the noise.

"Let their powers fuel my own. Let us all have powers grown!"

Instantly, Terra disappeared. Two seconds later, the amulet was ripped from around the older woman's neck, and she sputtered in surprise. Delilah brought her hands to her head and closed her eyes. With one last shout of defiance, the evil witch crumpled to the floor. All the books and lamps and knickknacks that were in midflight dropped to the ground, shattering and littering the place with more debris. Terra reappeared right next to Aura and handed over the amulet.

"Nice work," Delilah said.

"We have it!" Aura cried, lifting the necklace into the air. "We have the last amulet!"

Ruth barely registered what Aura was saying. "What was she going on about?" she asked shakily. "Were we here a few months ago? Did we save her from some demon?"

"Come on. Why would we save an evil

witch?" Delilah asked. "The woman was clearly cuckoo."

"It doesn't matter what she said," Aura told her. "We got what we came for. Now let's get home and reunite the amulets."

Delilah, grinning like mad, practically skipped out of the trashed apartment, leaving the woman's prone form behind. Even Terra, who had seemed almost forlorn on the way to Maribel's, looked pleased with herself over the accomplished mission. Ruth followed after them slowly, taking one look back at the broken witch. Something about the look the woman had in her eyes before she went down made Ruth's blood run cold. She had looked as if she truly believed what she was saying. She had seemed completely and utterly betrayed.

Her nerves frayed, Ruth stepped out of the apartment and closed the door gently behind her. Something wasn't right here. She just wished she could figure out what it was.

"It's not like they had time to brainwash her, so it has to be a spell," Piper said, walking back and forth in front of the Book of Shadows.

"They must have used a few," Leo said. "It sounds like they gave Phoebe amnesia, protected their house from your power, *and* they must have also cloaked it *and* Phoebe. Otherwise, I would have been able to sense her, and you guys would have been able to scry."

"Strong spells," Paige said, chewing on the inside of her cheek. She sat on the settee in the center of the attic, looking up at her sister and brother-in-law. "These girls really know what they're doing."

"Well, not entirely," Piper said. "Because if they did, then they would have known better than to mess with us."

"Someone's pissed off," Paige said with a smirk.

"Yeah, well, you mess with my sister, you mess with me," Piper said, stepping up in front of the Book. "Okay. We don't have to worry about the cloaking spells. All we need to do is figure out a way to reverse their nifty little amnesia spell," Piper said, flipping a few of the heavy pages. "Once Phoebe wakes up and remembers who she is, she'll get out of there herself."

"If she can," Paige said.

"Of course she can," Piper said.

"Okay, fine," Paige said, standing and pushing her hands into the back pockets of her jeans. "There's only one problem with this plan."

"What's that?" Piper asked.

"Well, you're not going to be able to reverse the spell without knowing the spell," Paige said. "Not if it's that strong. You'll need to use their words and twist them to reverse it."

Piper's heart sank and she pushed her hands into her hair. "That's right. Why didn't I think of that?"

"Because you're in a panic and all you can think about is fixing this," Leo said, walking over to her. He put his hands on her shoulders and kneaded the tight muscles. "Take a deep breath and try to relax. You need to concentrate."

"What I need is their spell," Piper said, slapping her hands down on the Book.

"Well, then, let's go get it," Paige said. She walked over and took Piper's hand.

"But how? We already tried to get in there and it resulted in several head injuries, as you might recall," Piper told her. Her head was, in fact, still throbbing in several places, even though Leo had healed her.

"That was when we were doing it your way," Paige said, squeezing her fingers. "Let's try my way."

"It's worth a shot," Piper said with a sigh. "You'll take care of our magical visitors?" she asked Leo.

"Sure," he said. "They've been pretty quiet since the last battle anyway. Just . . . be careful."

"Always," Piper said.

Then she and Paige orbed out.

Paige reconstituted in the center of a plush, modern living room. All around her were pristine white couches with colorful pillows strewn over them. Not at all what she had expected. Evil beings' lairs were usually more gothic and dark and creepy.

"Are we in the right place?" she asked, even though she trusted her orbing instincts completely.

Piper walked around the thick throw rug and paused at one of the side tables. She lifted a framed photo and held it out to Paige. "I'd say so."

Paige's jaw dropped. It was a picture of Phoebe with her arms thrown around the three evil witches. She immediately recognized Phoebe's pose—the image had been lifted from the photo that used to sit in the manor's entryway. The one of Phoebe, Piper, and Prue taken many years ago—before Paige had even known the Halliwells existed, let alone that they were related.

"Those witches stole our stuff!" Paige said, then took a closer look at the photo. There wasn't a trace of a line or any fuzziness whatsoever. "And someone is *really* good at Photoshop."

"No wonder they have her so convinced she belongs with them," Piper said. "They really did their homework. I just can't believe you were actually able to orb in here."

"Yeah, well, it's a lot tougher to protect against a Whitelighter's power than it is a witch's power," Paige said with a blithe shrug. "Guess they forgot we had *that* working for us."

"Still, it was a little rash," Piper said, looking around. "What if they had all been here?"

"Then we would have fought them," Paige

said, feeling a rush of frustration. "Why are you always picking on me? I got us in here, didn't I?"

"Look, I'm just trying to keep you alive, okay?" Piper said, stepping toward a pair of double doors at the back of the room.

"I can do that just fine on my own, thanks," Paige said sarcastically.

"So far, anyway," Piper said under her breath.

"I appreciate the vote of confidence." Paige took a deep breath and blew it out. "You know what? Let's not fight. We have to find that spell and get out of here before those witches *do* come home."

"Good point," Piper said, grasping the door handles. "Let's see what's in here."

She pushed the doors open and a whoosh of cool air greeted them. The room inside was dim thanks to thick curtains covering all the windows. Set up in the center of the floor were four large pillows, and a few Asian tapestries hung from the dark walls. At first it seemed as if that was all there was to the room, but as Paige's eyes adjusted, she saw a wall cupboard and a trunk in the far corner.

"That looks promising," she said, pointing at the trunk.

Piper walked over and tried the trunk's latch, but it didn't budge.

"Locked," she said. "Stand back."

Paige did as she was told and Piper blasted the trunk's lock into a billion pieces. They both knelt in front of it and opened the heavy lid.

"Jackpot," Piper said.

Paige had to agree. Inside were dozens of candles, a mortar and pestle, bags and bags of herbs and weeds and flower petals, and bottles full of eye-of-newt, salamander claws, and other magical ingredients. Piper pulled out a black notebook that had papers and Post-Its sticking out of it at all angles. She opened it and Paige looked over her shoulder. The very first page held a simple lost-and-found spell. Very basic.

"It's like their very own Book of Shadows," Paige said.

"Please let the spell be in here," Piper said.

She flipped to the back and found the most recent spell. Paige saw that someone had worked pretty hard on it, crossing out entire lines and paragraphs and making notes in the margins. But words like *memory* and *new life* jumped out at her.

"This has to be it," she said. "Check the back of the page."

Piper flipped the page over and there it was, written out in a messy scrawl. The title of the spell was "Phoebe Project."

"Very specific," Piper said sardonically.

"Well, well, well! Look who's here!"

Paige's heart lodged in her throat, and both she and Piper jumped up. Piper handed the spell book to Paige behind her back, and Paige clutched it in her suddenly sweaty fingers.

Aura, Phoebe, and their two friends were guarding the double doorway, lined up and ready to fight. Paige's eyes went directly to Phoebe, and she felt a little flutter of hope. Was it just her, or was Phoebe not looking quite as confident as she had earlier? Could it be that she was starting to question the people she was with?

"How did we not hear them come in?" Paige asked under her breath.

"Stealthy little suckers," Piper responded quietly. "Look, we don't want any trouble," she told the witches. "Just let us have our sister back and we'll call it even."

"Oooh, what are you, scared of us now?" Aura said, stepping forward. "Well, you should be."

She lifted her hand, and Paige instantly flew into the air, her arms flailing out at her sides. The dark-haired girl's eyes widened.

"She has the spell book!" the girl shouted.

"Time to go!" Piper announced.

She flicked her fingers at the doors behind the witches and they exploded into kindling. The force of the blast sent all four witches flying forward, including Phoebe, who landed on one of the fat floor pillows. Released from Aura's power, Paige careened toward earth.

"Let's get out of here," Piper said, grabbing her hand.

"But what about Phoebe?" Paige asked, reaching toward her other sister.

"We have to reverse the spell or she'll never come back to us," Piper said. "Go!"

From the corner of her eye, Paige saw the dark-haired girl rousing herself. She still had no idea what that chick's power was, but she had a feeling she didn't want to find out. Casting a hopeless glance at Phoebe, she held the spell book to her chest, grabbed Piper's arm, and orbed out.

Back in the attic at the manor, Paige tossed the spell book onto the couch and turned to face Piper. "I don't understand why you wouldn't let me bring Phoebe with us."

"If my instincts are right, Phoebe will be here soon enough," Piper said, grabbing the book and opening it to the back page. "They'll be coming for this. They'll be coming for *us*. We just have to be ready for them when they do."

Paige sighed and looked at the floor. "Thanks for saving my butt back there," she said reluctantly. "Maybe I do need your help staying alive . . . sometimes."

Piper smiled. "No problem. And thank you for being bold enough to charge in there so that we could get *this*," she said, opening the evil trio's spell book atop the Book of Shadows. "Now let's get to work."

Chapter 11

"How the hell did they get in here?" Aura ranted, whirling on Terra and Delilah. "I thought we had the house protected!"

"I told you they would find a way in," Terra said, holding herself as if she were trying to keep from breaking down. "I told you!"

"Shut up, Terra," Delilah snapped. "No one likes a girl who says 'I told you so.'"

"Well, I *did*," Terra said, pouting. "You guys never want to listen to me."

Ruth watched the argument unfold, feeling a sense of uneasiness. She had never seen the three of them fight like this. But she supposed they were just upset about being ambushed in their own home. She was pretty upset about it herself.

"It doesn't matter how they got in," Delilah said, crossing to the cabinet on the wall. There was a menacing glint in her dark eyes. "All that matters now is that they're going to pay."

Aura took a deep breath and stepped forward, a serene smile lighting her face. She took the chain with the key from around her neck and handed it to Delilah.

"That's right," she said. "Now that we have the fourth amulet, they'll never be able to bother us again."

"What do you mean?" Ruth asked, walking over to join them.

Aura and Delilah exchanged a long look. Slowly, Delilah opened the cabinet. She lifted out the first amulet and handed it to Aura. Aura slipped the black chord over her head and rested the amulet against her chest, touching it reverently with her fingertips.

"We weren't just gathering the amulets to keep them away from evil," Aura told Ruth calmly. "We were gathering them because once they're reunited, their power is paramount. If four witches with powers like ours wear the amulets, those four witches will be unstoppable."

Ruth's heart began to pound in a shallow, nervous beat. Delilah placed the second amulet around her own neck. She then lifted the third from the cabinet and handed it to Terra. Terra's hands were shaking as she fastened the beaded necklace around her own neck. Then Aura turned to Ruth.

"And now, this one is for you," she said.

Ruth stared at the amulet. It was the one that

Terra had ripped from the neck of the last witch—the witch that had somehow recognized her. For some reason, she felt nothing but fear. She wasn't entirely sure that she wanted to take on the power Aura had described.

"We've worked for this for a long time, Ruth," Aura said. "You might not remember it all, but it's true. You wanted this as much as we did. Maybe even more," she added.

Ruth swallowed hard. Her throat was dry. She looked around at her friends. They stared back at her steadily, waiting. Waiting for her to join them.

"It'll be fine, Ruth," Aura said, holding out the amulet on its brown leather chord. "It's going to be amazing."

Ruth nodded. She had to do this. If she didn't, then what had the last two days been for? All those battles, all that danger, all that work. Clearly, they had been working toward this. She couldn't let her friends down.

Her fingers trembling, she reached for the amulet. Somehow, she got those fingers to tie the leather chord around her neck. The moment it was fastened and the cool metal of the amulet touched her skin, an incredible warmth overcame her. It infused her with an intense sense of calm, of confidence, of power. Ruth looked at her friends and saw that each of their amulets was glowing with bright white light. She looked down at her own necklace, to see that it was glowing as well.

"Do you feel that?" Aura asked, grinning.

"Try your power," Delilah urged.

Aura lifted her hand, and the trunk in the corner shot into the air so fast it slammed into the ceiling and shattered, spilling bottles and bags and spells all over the floor. Ruth jumped back, startled, but then slowly began to smile. That was some power.

"Oops," Aura said with a giggle.

"Nice one." Delilah laughed.

"Terra?" Aura said.

She had disappeared. A moment later, Ruth felt a hand on the back of her head and her hair flip up. Then the same thing happened to Aura, and then Delilah's braids went flying. Terra finally reappeared, laughing giddily.

"Very mature," Aura teased.

"I've never been able to do that without the empowerment spell before," Terra said happily.

"Ruth?" Aura said.

"What?" Ruth asked uncertainly.

"Try getting a premonition," Delilah said. "I'll bet you can get one without touching a thing."

"How?" Ruth asked, smiling. She was starting to feel their excitement. It was infectious.

"Just think about something. Think about the Giants," Delilah suggested. "They're playing the Dodgers tomorrow. What's the final score?"

Ruth closed her eyes and thought of the baseball team's orange and black uniforms. Within seconds she saw the scoreboard in her mind. Heard the announcer calling out the score. Saw the spectators leaving the stadium.

"Five-four, Dodgers," she said with a grin, opening her eyes.

She hadn't even felt the shock that she normally felt when her premonitions came on. And, coming out of it, there was none of the dizziness or disorientation.

"Damn," Delilah said under her breath. "Why did I bet on the Giants?"

"Are you going to try your power?" Ruth asked her.

"Can't," Delilah said, shrugging her shoulders. "Not without knocking one of you guys out. But I can tell you that Terra's thinking about spying on her ex-boyfriend with her invisibility powers," she added with a sly smile.

"Delilah! Get out of my head!" Terra said, blushing.

"And *Aura* is thinking about attacking the evil witches," Delilah said. "A little payback, perhaps?"

"You don't need magical powers to know that's what *I'm* thinking about," Aura said with a laugh. She crossed to the cabinet and pulled out a piece of paper that was sitting on the bottom. "Good thing we didn't keep this in the spell book."

"What is it?" Ruth asked.

"It's a spell," Aura told her, unfolding the

page. "A spell that should strip those witches of their powers once and for all."

Ruth's heart skipped a beat. *Another battle.* She had thought they were done with that for a while.

"It's time to go on the offensive, ladies," Aura announced, handing Delilah the spell. "Memorize that. All of you. We're going to need it."

"What are we going to do?" Ruth asked.

"They attack us in our house, we're going to attack them in theirs," Aura said.

"But we can't go there," Ruth said, her mouth suddenly dry. "That's where my first premonition took place. That's where I saw you guys . . ."

"Die?" Aura said as Delilah gave the spell to Terra. "Don't worry, Ruth. That's not going to happen."

"How can you be so sure?" Ruth asked.

"Because you got that premonition before we had the power of the amulets," Delilah told her. "Trust us. With these on our side, no one can stop us."

"Take the spell, Ruth," Aura said as Terra held it out to her. "Take it and memorize it. It's time to take those witches down, and we can't do it without you."

Ruth took the spell from Terra and read it over. It was short and to the point, and, somehow, with the power of the amulet coursing through her veins, Ruth had no doubt that it would work. In her mind's eye she saw the two evil witches helpless and cowering, knowing they had met their match.

"Fine," she said grimly. "Let's get this over with."

"All done," Paige told Piper, handing over the spell she had just finished copying out on a clean sheet of paper. "Think it'll do the trick?"

Piper scanned the page quickly, then compared it to the spell in the back of the evil witches' book. "Sounds good to me. Nice job, Paige."

"Please. We did it together," Paige said, shoving her chair back and standing. "Let's just hope we don't have to be in the same room with her for it to work."

"No negative energy, please," Piper said. "Let's do this thing."

They held up the sheet of paper, Piper's hand clutching one side, Paige's the other, their free hands clasped together between them. As Piper opened her mouth to recite the spell, a loud crash sounded from downstairs.

"Oh, crap," she said. "The Flecters are back."

There was a scream that sounded a bit like one of the nymphs. Piper's heart jumped into her throat.

"Let's go," Paige said.

Together, they ran out of the attic and down the stairs. Piper shoved the new spell into her back pocket and lifted her hands, ready to blast

the first Flecter she saw. But when she got to the
bottom of the steps, she stopped in her tracks
and her hands instantly fell. It wasn't the
Flecters who were battling the magical contin-
gent.

It was Phoebe.

"What the hell is that thing?" Ruth shouted as
some tiny man in green shot power at her from a
rickety-looking cane.

A huge man in a smelly pelt swung his arm at
Terra's head. Instantly, Terra vanished, reappear-
ing behind him a moment later. The man looked
around dumbly as Terra lifted a mirror off the
wall and cracked it over his head. His eyes
rolled up and he fell forward, nearly taking
Delilah down with him. Delilah slipped out of
the way just in time, and as the giant hit the
floor, the entire house shook.

"What's going on in this freak house?"
Delilah asked.

"Forget about them!" Aura shouted, levitating some pretty girl in green to the ceiling and
leaving her there. "There are the witches! We
have to do the spell!"

Sure enough, the two evil witches were
standing at the bottom of the stairs—and they
looked completely dumbstruck. Ruth stood up
quickly and took Delilah's hand. Delilah
grabbed Aura and Aura reached for Terra,
pulling Terra's trembling form to her.

"Ready?" Aura asked.

All four amulets glowed white and warm. Ruth felt the power take over and knew that the other girls felt it as well. She could somehow sense their confidence and determination, as if the amulets solidified their connection.

"Ready," they all replied.

"What are they doing?" Paige asked. "They're not gonna levitate us again, are they?"

"Come on," Piper said, reaching for Paige's hand. "We have to recite the spell."

She knew that if she could just give Phoebe back her memory, this whole nightmare would be over.

"These two witches that we see, let their powers no longer be," Phoebe and her friends recited.

"Oh, my God! Piper! Blast them!" Paige cried.

"No. We have to do the spell," Piper said, grasping Paige's fingers.

"There's no time. They're trying to strip our powers!"

"Take from them that which helps them fight, let their powers flee into the night," the four witches cried.

Piper lifted her hands and shot her power at the petite girl on the far end. Nothing happened. She felt nothing. No sizzle in her fingertips, no burst of warmth. Her power was gone.

"Oh, this is not good," Paige said, looking up.

Piper followed her sister's gaze and saw hundreds of white orbs rising toward the sky above her head. More orbs rose up from Paige's body, heading straight for the ceiling.

"Hey! That's my power!" Piper shouted.

"Not anymore," Aura said with an evil smile.

Piper watched helplessly as the orbs shot up through the ceiling and into the ether, taking her power with them. She looked at Phoebe and her new band of witches. For the first time in a very long time, Piper felt like a sitting duck.

"Kill the witches," Aura said with a sneer.

"Leo!" Piper shouted.

Instantly, Leo orbed down from Wyatt's room, right between the two lines of witches. He looked at Piper with a question in his eyes.

"A little help?" Piper said. "We're kind of out of power."

"What?" Leo blurted. He tried to grab the dark-haired witch as she stepped forward, but the girl took one look at Leo and he crumpled lifelessly to the ground.

"Sweet!" Delilah said. "It works!"

"Leo!" Piper cried.

"Watch out!" Paige shouted, shoving Piper into the living room.

Piper looked up just as Aura lifted her hand. She jumped behind what was left of the couch before the girl's power could take hold of her. Paige dove down next to her as Teague and the other magical creatures launched into battle mode.

"What the hell is going on?" Piper demanded.

"Looks like their powers have grown," Paige said.

"Ya think?" Piper cried.

"They're all wearing the amulets. Did you see?" Paige said. "They must augment their powers somehow."

"Great. They've got magical batteries around their necks and we've completely lost our powers," Piper said, sitting up. "What are we supposed to do now?"

"Don't worry. We've got something better than amulets on our side," Paige said as all the leprechauns raced forward as one. "We've got friends."

A band of fairies rushed around the witches' heads, tossing their hair into their eyes, confusing them. A troll ran out from a corner of the room and raced around Aura's feet in a blur, upending her. She crashed to the floor on her butt and let out a loud cry of pain.

"That *is* a good thing," Piper said with a smile. "Just don't hurt Phoebe!" she cried as a lamp crashed to the floor in front of her.

"Where's the spell?" Paige asked.

Piper groped for her back pocket and struggled to pull out the spell. Paige shouted in surprise as one of the leprechauns skittered across the floor and slammed into the wall in front of them, knocked out.

"We have to stop this," she said.

"We will," Piper said. "You ready?"

Paige nodded resolutely. "Go!"

Together, they stood up and faced Phoebe. The dark-haired witch was on the ground and Aura was busy with the satyr and the nymphs. The third witch was nowhere to be seen. But their sister came right at them, as if ready to launch herself into the air and take them both down.

"Powers that be, help our sister see. Bring back her every memory," Piper and Paige recited quickly. "Let her new life fade away, and bring her back to her true way."

Phoebe aimed a roundhouse kick at Paige's head and let out a screeching battle cry. Paige ducked and Phoebe whirled in a circle, her leg hitting nothing but air. Thrown off balance, she staggered backward into the wall behind her, her eyes closed.

"Did it work?" Paige asked from the floor as the battle raged all around her.

Phoebe shook her head, clearly disoriented. Her fingertips were pressed against the wall behind her, clinging for dear life.

"I'm not sure," Piper said.

Finally, Phoebe opened her eyes. Paige stood slowly, peeking out from behind the couch. Phoebe looked from Piper to Paige and back again. Her skin was waxy and pale, as if she were about to throw up. She looked as though she had just seen her entire life flash before her eyes.

"Phoebe?" Piper said hopefully.

"Piper? Paige?" Phoebe said, blinking. "What's going on?"

Chapter 12

"Phoebe! You're back!" Piper cried, as a blast of leprechaun rainbow shot past her head and shattered the window behind her. "What do you remember?"

All at once, Phoebe Halliwell's entire life came back to her in a rush. Her childhood as the baby of the family, her rebellious teenage years, her grandmother, her sisters, her boyfriends, her disastrous, doomed marriage to a demon. Those people in the photo in her "room" were not her parents. Her parents hadn't died in a car accident. Her father was actually still alive. And she hadn't gone to UC San Francisco. Nor was she an unemployed English teacher. She was an advice columnist and a witch. A good witch. One of the three most powerful witches in the world.

It was all a huge, tremendous relief. She knew who she was! She was not Ruth Miller, some random goddess-worshipping Wicca. She was

Phoebe Halliwell, one of the Charmed Ones. She couldn't believe how incredibly reassuring it was just to have memories.

Then her memory of the last few days hit her like an anvil to the head. Phoebe's eyes widened and her hand flew to her mouth. "Oh, no! I stripped your powers!" she said, rushing forward. "I am so, *so* sorry!"

"It's okay," Paige said. "Can you reverse it?"

"I think so," Phoebe said. "I just need to—"

Aura stormed into the room, her hair and clothes tossed around from the force of all the powers and spells that were circulating the manor. Her eyes smoldered with hatred as she took in the three reunited sisters.

"Oh, no, you don't," she shouted at Phoebe. "You're one of *us* now. Whether you like it or not."

"Phoebe! Watch out!" Paige cried.

But it was too late. Aura raised her hand into the air, flinging Phoebe off her feet and toward the ceiling. Piper automatically reached out to blast the girl, but nothing happened. Her powers were still out there somewhere, useless to her.

"Aura! Let me down!" Phoebe cried.

"Why? So you can vanquish us? I don't think so!" Aura cried.

Suddenly, one of the leprechaun's flying rainbows hit the giant. He woke with a start, saw Phoebe hovering in the air above him, and glanced at Aura. With one quick grab he

snatched Aura's ankle, and she went sprawling
on the floor. Phoebe shouted and dropped to the
ground, landing on her feet.

"Nice move," Piper commented.

"I'm used to levitating, remember?" Phoebe
said. She turned around to find Delilah attempting to knock out a muse with her power. Delilah
kept narrowing her eyes over and over again
while the muse just stood there, smiling back at
her, letting the girl keep trying in vain.

"Why isn't it working?" Delilah cried, throwing out her hands.

"Hey, newbie!" Phoebe yelled.

Delilah turned around, and the second she
did, Phoebe hit her with an uppercut to the nose.
There was a loud *crack* and Delilah's eyes rolled
back into her head before she hit the floor.

"Why wasn't her power working on you?"
Piper asked the muse.

She lifted one translucent shoulder. "I'm not
corporeal. If she'd kept going, she would have
knocked *herself* out eventually. She should have
known that. Amateur."

"Well, that's two down," Phoebe said.

She whirled around on Terra, who was
cowering in the corner by the door, looking like
she very much wanted to be anywhere but here.
The second Phoebe looked at her, she yelped in
fear, went invisible, and ripped her amulet off.
Instantly, she reappeared.

"Oops," she said, looking at the amulet.

She threw it on the ground. "I'm outta here."

Then she turned and raced out the front door as fast as her sandaled feet would take her.

"Are you going after her?" Piper asked.

"Nah. She's pretty harmless," Phoebe said. "Especially without this," she added, picking up the fallen amulet.

"Give that back, you witch!" Aura cried, struggling on the floor.

The giant had her pinned under one of his large feet, and she was squirming around like a fish that had just been tossed onto the deck of a boat.

"You can let her up," Phoebe said to the giant.

He shrugged and lifted his foot. Aura shoved herself to her feet and faced off with Phoebe.

"That was a big mistake, witch," she said, lifting her hand.

Phoebe levitated half an inch off the ground, then gently landed again. Aura's face dropped and her skin turned ashen.

"Feeling a little powerless without your girls, Aura?" Phoebe asked, stepping toward her. "I can already feel the power draining out of *my* amulet. I don't think your little plan is going to work."

"Your sisters don't have their powers," Aura said. "I can still take you on."

Phoebe looked at Piper and Paige. "Right. I should do something about that, shouldn't I?" She took a deep breath and centered herself in front of her sisters. "These two witches that I love, bring back their powers from above."

"What're you doing? You don't have enough power to reverse our spell!" Aura cried.

"Bring back that which helps them fight, let their powers be set to right," Phoebe finished calmly.

"No!" Aura cried as the orbs reappeared above Piper and Paige.

The orbs shot down and into the sisters, and for a moment they were both aglow with their restored power. Piper smiled at Phoebe as Paige orbed in and out, grinning.

"That feels *so* much better," Paige said.

"You can't do this to me!" Aura cried, lunging at Phoebe. "I won't let you."

Phoebe smirked, pulled her arm back, and flattened her with a right hook to the jaw. Aura spun around and hit the ground with a satisfying thud.

"That's for naming me Ruth," she said to the girl's prone form.

"Shall we?" Piper asked, reaching for Phoebe's hand.

"The spell to vanquish an evil soul?" Phoebe suggested.

"Or two," Paige said, glancing at Delilah's unconscious body.

"Right," Phoebe said.

"Evil witches in my sight, vanquish thy-selves, vanquish thy might, in this and every future life," Phoebe, Piper and Paige recited.

In a flash of light, both of the witches were gone, leaving nothing but their magical amulets behind. The giant fell forward slightly as Aura disappeared from under his foot, but he quickly righted himself with an embarrassed smile.

"Is *thyselves* even a word?" Paige asked, looking around at her sisters.

"Who cares? It worked!" Piper said.

"You guys, I am so sorry!" Phoebe cried, reaching for both of them and pulling them in for a hug. "I can't believe I was fighting against you. How could I not remember?"

"They cast a powerful spell on you," Paige said, resting her head on Phoebe's shoulder.

"It doesn't matter now," Piper said. "All that matters is that you're back."

Suddenly, Leo roused himself from the floor, groaning in pain. "What happened?" he asked, bringing his hand to his head as he sat.

"Leo!" Piper cried, dropping to the floor. "Oh, honey! Are you okay?" she asked, touching his temple gently.

"I think so," he said. "Did you say something about losing your powers?"

"Yeah. But we got them back," Piper said, flipping her hair over her shoulder as she looked up at her sisters. "Thanks to Phoebe."

Leo smiled. "You're Phoebe again?"

"Yep. No more Ruth. Ruth—blech!" Phoebe said, sticking out her tongue. "How could they give me a name like that?"

"Don't worry," Paige said, wrapping her arm around Phoebe's waist. "*We'll* never call you that."

"It's so good to be home," Phoebe said. Then she actually took in her surroundings—the trashed furniture, the shards of glass and ceramic everywhere, the smashed mirror in the foyer, and the dozens of magical creatures nursing wounds or just waking up from Delilah's former power. "Even if it is a big trash heap," she added.

At that moment, at least twenty Flecter demons shimmered in all over the manor, surrounding the sisters and all their magical friends.

"Okay. So maybe I spoke too soon," Phoebe said, backing instinctively toward the door.

"Paige! The spell!" Piper cried as each of the demons raised an energy ball over his head. Their yellow eyes glowed with malice, drool dripping from their pointed teeth.

"Let's get out of here first!" Leo shouted, grabbing Piper's hand.

"Good plan!"

Paige grabbed Phoebe and they all orbed out to the kitchen together, just as the energy balls flew. Phoebe pressed her hands against the cool surface of the kitchen island and caught her breath.

"Close call," she said, as dozens of explosions shook the house.

"Leo, grab the potions!" Piper shouted to be heard over the battle.

Leo plucked three bottles from the counter. Phoebe could tell that the potion had been brewed recently because the pot was still congealing on the stove and there were ingredients everywhere. What had gone on around here in her absence? She didn't have time to ask. Leo handed each of them a vial, then stepped back.

"Here—recite this!" Paige demanded, slapping a piece of crumpled paper down on the counter.

Phoebe didn't even need to ask what it was. When one of her sisters told her to recite something in the heat of battle, she just did it. Together, she, Piper, and Paige gathered around the spell.

"By the force of Heaven and Hell, draw to us this demon's lair. So that we may vanquish this evil, help us find him, take us there."

Phoebe felt a sudden yank, as if her entire body had just been plucked skyward by some invisible hand. She felt as if she were on some psychotic, invisible roller coaster. The world spun before her, a dizzying rush of insane colors, and then, as quickly as it had all begun, her feet were back on solid ground.

"Whoa," Phoebe said.

It took her brain a moment to catch up with the rest of her, but when it did, she was looking at a dirty, smelly demon sitting on an ornate throne. All around him, Flecters milled about, looking toward the rock ceiling high above as if waiting to be called into battle.

"The emperor?" Phoebe asked.

"I'm hoping," Piper replied.

"How did you get here?" the Flecter emperor demanded, sitting forward.

Instantly, all the Flecters in the room turned, and with a universal growl, they descended upon the sisters.

"Now!" Piper shouted, tossing her potion at the emperor's feet.

Phoebe and Paige did the same, then dropped to the ground and took cover. There was an incredible, deafening scream, and then a huge blast of searing heat shot through the cave. Phoebe struggled for breath and clung to her sisters as the cries of the Flecters echoed against the stone walls. When the heat finally subsided, Phoebe cautiously looked up. The cave was completely empty. There were scorch marks everywhere, smoke swirling up into the air.

"They're gone," she said.

"Do you think the ones back home died too?" Paige asked.

Piper took their hands. "Only one way to find out."

Paige orbed the sisters home, and the moment Phoebe rematerialized in the living room, she knew that the vanquish had worked. The place was in even worse shape than it had been when they left, but there wasn't a Flecter to be seen.

"Everyone all right?" Piper called out.

Leo stepped out from behind the television armoire in the sunroom and glanced around the doorway.

"Fine," he said. All over the manor, leprechauns, muses, fairies, and nymphs came out from cover and dusted themselves off, looking dazed.

"Now it's *really* good to be home," Phoebe said.

"Aren't you all so glad you came for counseling this weekend?" Piper asked the crowd.

"Oh, my God! That's why you're all here! I completely forgot," Phoebe cried, bringing her hand to her head. "Oh, no! You came here for help and all you did was end up fighting demons!"

"It's all right," a blond leprechaun said, reaching for his lady's hand. "The family that fights evil together, stays together."

"You got that right," Piper said, smiling at her sisters.

Leo joined them, pulling the three amulets out of his pocket. "I found these on the floor," he said, holding them out. "What do you want me to do with them?"

Phoebe was amazed by how harmless the little tokens looked resting in Leo's palm. But she knew that when they were united, they packed some serious punch. She had a feeling that, wherever they had come from, they had been divided amongst various witches for a reason. Good witches, she realized now.

"We should probably get them back to their rightful owners," she said, removing the fourth amulet from around her own neck. She handed it to Leo. "With a huge apology."

"I'm on it," Leo said, orbing out.

"Well, I guess we should get to work," Phoebe said, looking around at their magical friends. "I promised you guys I would help you, so if you're still interested . . ."

"That's all right," Teague said, stepping forward. His hat was gone and the bottoms of his corduroy pants had been burned off, but otherwise, he seemed okay. "I think we've all learned that there are bigger problems out there than our petty differences."

The magical creatures all nodded and mumbled their agreement.

"Besides," Teague said, dropping his voice to a whisper. "This place is not safe!"

Phoebe laughed. "Well, if you ever decide you do need me, feel free to come back," she said. "I really do feel badly about what happened."

"We were glad to help," the giant said with a bow.

Then, each of the creatures left the manor in their own magical way. The fairies flitted off through the destroyed windows, the muses dissolved, and the nymphs surrounded the giant and they all disappeared in a swirl of flowers, taking the satyr along with them. In a few minutes, everyone was gone, and Phoebe and her sisters were left in peace. In a house that looked like it had just been hit by a nuclear blast.

"Guess we should clean up, then," Phoebe said.

"Oh, no!" Paige told her, coming over and taking her arm. "Not you. *You* are going on vacation."

"Yes!" Piper agreed. "We think you need to take a few days off. Drive along the coast. Find a bed and breakfast. Kick your feet up and stay off them for a while."

"What are you guys talking about?" Phoebe asked, her brow knitting.

"Your life! It's insane!" Piper said. "You've got Elyse calling and me making you babysit all the time—"

"And the shopping and the vanquishing and the keeping up on the Book of Shadows," Paige added. "You're the only one who knew off the top of your head what the Flecters were. How much studying do you *do* up there?"

"And then there's the writing and the *counseling*," Piper said. "We never realized exactly how full your plate was."

"So we think you should take that vacation you were talking about," Paige told her. "We can take care of things around here, no problem."

They all looked around at the destruction that had occurred in Phoebe's absence.

"Yeah. Sure looks that way," Phoebe joked.

"What? We're all alive," Piper said. "That's what matters."

"Well, thanks, you guys," Phoebe said, truly touched. "But, to be honest, I just kind of had a vacation from my life and, well, it sort of sucked."

"But that's not a fair gauge," Piper told her. "You had a trio of evil witches making you do their bidding."

"True," Phoebe said. "But even when I wasn't helping out Aura, I knew something wasn't right. And I think it's just that I like my life. I like doing all that stuff you just mentioned. I like . . . being me."

"You do?" Paige asked.

"Don't sound so surprised," Phoebe said. "I just . . . maybe need to take it easy once in a while, that's all."

"Okay. How about you start right now?" Piper suggested, hooking her arm over Phoebe's shoulder and guiding her toward the stairs. "Why don't you go up to your room, change into your favorite silk pj's and relax? We'll take care of everything down here."

"You're sure?" Phoebe asked, her foot already climbing the first stair.

"We're sure," Paige told her. "You've more than earned it."

"Thanks, guys," Phoebe said. "Sounds like heaven."

When she was halfway up the stairs, Phoebe heard the phone ring. All her senses went promptly on alert, just like they always did at the sound of a phone. She paused and listened in as Piper answered.

"Oh, yes! *Hi*, Elyse!" Piper said. "No, no, she's not here. Phoebe has *left* the building. Yes . . . yes, of course I'll tell her. No, it won't do you any good to call her on her cell phone. She lost it. Yes! She did! I know. She is *so* irresponsible," Piper said, hamming it up.

Phoebe laughed and rolled her eyes. With a sigh, she turned and walked into her room, closing the door softly behind her. It was comforting to know that her sisters were there to take care of her, that they always would be. The next time she got stressed out or felt overwhelmed, she had to remember that. All she had to do was truly talk to her sisters and let them know how she was feeling, and they would work out the problem together. How could she have forgotten that?

Took a little amnesia to wake me up, Phoebe thought with a smile, savoring the irony.

She climbed into her bed and sank into the soft satin sheets. For the first time in days, Phoebe felt like herself again. *This* was her home. This was where she belonged.

About the Author

Emma Harrison is an editor turned writer who has written many books for the Charmed series. She lives in New Jersey with her husband.